I0537973

MisIntentions

Written by:

T. Lee Moore

Cover design created by T. Lee Moore
Cover Artwork by T. Lee Moore
Cover created by Kathy@signsbymilsoft.com
Text copyright© 2012 T. Lee Moore

You can contact the author at her website:

www.mooregrimtales.com

Chapter 1

Mara woke Sunday morning, and realized she was home to stay. This was not her usual weekend visit with her dad, where she would pack her things to return to GG's.

Her Great Grandmother, affectionately referred to as GG, was gone, passed on to the next life. Her father had arranged for her to start school tomorrow and they laid GG to rest yesterday. They had both been exhausted when they arrived home last night so her belongings were waiting to be unloaded from the truck.

She sat up in bed, stretched, and looked up at the mobile of colorful butterflies she created several years ago, an act of hope that this return home would have happened sooner. Each butterfly wing contained a message for her mother. She would imagine them flying out the window to deliver them. She put her legs over the side of the bed and slipped into her pink fuzzy slippers.

Her dad was already in the kitchen when she got downstairs and she could smell cinnamon. "Mmm, Dad, you made my favorite!" A breakfast she called 'dirty bread' as a little girl. She grabbed a plate from the cabinet then loaded it with three pieces of French toast.

He watched as she drowned her toast in syrup and then laughed, "Well, we've got a lot of stuff to unload and a little sugar boost will put some fuel in your tank."

"Oh, Dad, I don't really have that much stuff."

Her grandmother's house was small and congested from years of collected items, allowing Mara little room to have much of anything. Her belongings fit into six medium-sized cardboard moving boxes. Other than clothes, a bit of make-up, a hair dryer and some other personal care items, she only had a box of CD's, a portable player and a personalclock/radio. Although technological advances had been made over the years, GG felt CD's and their players, clock radios and televisions with cable, oh yeah and the cordless house phones, were probably deadly enough without bringing in the 'new cancer causing agents' as she liked to call it. GG also believed when they started using actual cans to can foods, was the 'beginning of the end'. 'Mark my words,' she'd say, 'Cancers and illnesses are going to start striking people down. Those cans are just toxic and they'll rob the nutrients right out of the food.'

After they carried the boxes to her bedroom, she unpacked. She gladly threw her old school uniforms into a garbage bag. Never again would she wear khaki pants and Polo style shirts. The school she would start attending tomorrow didn't require them.

She unpacked the rest of her clothes adding each piece to its respective drawers until she got to the last item. A gallon sized freezer bag containing a small blue dress her mother made for her on her sixth birthday.

Nearly ten years had passed since her mother got into her car and drove away never to return or be found. She sat on her bed and carefully removed the little dress with its yellowing and tattered lace trim. As she held it out in front of her, she saw an image of her younger self and the events of that day returned as clear as if it were happening again...

At 3:30, she heard 'Uncle' Jack's cruiser crush the gravel road leading up to her house. She ran out the back door and didn't stop until she wrapped her arms tightly around his legs. He laughed and looked down at her placing a hand on her head. When she backed away and raised her face towards him, he lifted her in his arms and carried her to the back porch, "You sit right here young lady, Uncle Jack's gotta talk to your daddy." He pinched her nose between his thumb and forefinger and gave her a wink.

Once he entered the kitchen, Mara ran over to the open window, squatted beneath it and raised her face so that her eyes were just above the edge of the windowsill.

Sheriff Jack Norton walked behind the chair Ray occupied and placed a hand on his friend's shoulder to comfort him. He stood there briefly waiting for Ray's sobs to subside. When Ray calmed down some, Jack placed his hat on the table and moved to sit across from him. "Ray, I'm so sorry this is happening to you and Mara. Jenny and I are worried sick."

"Jack, I don't know what to do. She left here just before eleven to run to the store for some lunch stuff and that was it. I don't know where she is or why she hasn't called." Ray stood and walked across the kitchen running his hands through his hair. "I just can't...I don't understand. Is this really happening?"

"Did you two have a fight or anything?" Jack asked.

"No. I can't make sense of it. Everything was fine as far as I know, except she hasn't come back. I took Mara for a ride to the store and around the back roads considering the idea maybe the car broke down or something. The people at the store say they hadn't even seen her."

"Well I got Deputy Marks out there searching for her or the Mustang." Jack said.

Jack ran his hands over his crew cut and leaned back, taking a deep breath. "It's only been four months since the incident at her sister's. I know Kate and Ernie's deaths were disturbing and I know she didn't agree with the conclusion of the investigation." He looked toward Ray with deep concern in his eyes, "So let me ask you Ray, do you think she's gone up there? To the cabin?"

Her dad was leaning over the sink looking to the woods across the back yard. As he turned back toward the table, Mara ducked just below the windowsill but she continued to listen.

"I can't even imagine Nora wanting to return to that cabin Jack. The way everything was left there. I mean, no one's been up there since it happened and no one's wanted to see it. Why would she suddenly, now, today just go?" Ray dropped back into his chair. "What's happening Jack? Where is my wife?"

"Did you at least see which direction she was headed?" Jack asked.

"No. I was working on my truck and I never looked up. Just raised my hand with the socket wrench in it back towards her voice. She has been more quiet than usual lately and distant at times, but I never thought..."

Jack continued, "I know that incident at Ernie's and Katie's disturbed her, but was she doing or saying anything you can think of that would indicate she was having new problems dealing with it?"

Mara jumped when she heard her dad's fist hit the table. She lifted her head again to peek through the window and saw her father with his head on his arms, his body jerking as he cried. Mara had never seen her dad cry and it made her want to cry too but she knew Mommy would come home and then Daddy would be okay.

"I'm going to the station and make some phone calls to some neighboring counties. I need a picture for the press. Jenny's at the station, if you like I can take Mara and Jenny can watch her for a while?"

Ray raised his right hip slightly from his seat, removed his wallet from his rear pocket and took the picture of Nora from it, "No that's okay, I've already called GG and she's coming in town from Claramay. She's taking Mara home with her until Nora's back." When Mara heard a chair scrape the floor she ran over to the porch swing and took a seat, hoping it would seem she had been there the whole time. Jack looked to his left at her as he walked out the backdoor. He sat next to her, put his hat on and looked down at her. "You're going to your GG's, huh?"

"That's what Daddy told me. I don't want to though." Mara searched his face with inquisitive eyes. " Uncle Jack is Daddy gonna be okay?"

He tried to give her a reassuring smile but the heaviness of his heart only allowed a small weak one. "Oh baby I'm sure he will. We just have to figure some things out. So you go on with GG and I'll take care of your daddy." He pinched her nose again and winked, "It's gonna be okay."

"But I really want to stay here 'til Mommy gets home."

"Honey I don't know what time your momma's comin' home, but until she does you'd probably have more fun at your GG's." He hesitated then asked, "Don't ya think so?"

"I guess so, but as soon as my mommy comes back you make sure my daddy comes to get me."

"Baby when your mama gets home Uncle Jack will come get you right away and bring you home himself. How 'bout that?"

For the first few months, Mara waited by the big picture window in her GG's living room but Uncle Jack never came for her. GG and Father decided it would be best for grandmother to raise her. By the time she was twelve, she tried to talk them into letting her return home. Her father could raise her fine, she didn't need a woman to raise her just because she was a girl. But, by the time she was thirteen, it was apparent her father was afraid to let Mara go have a normal life. She was pretty sure the fear stemmed from the disappearance of her mother.

During her weekend visits, he would not let her out of his sight. Sometimes it made her angry with her mother. Years passed with unanswered questions. At times Mara would wonder if her mother was alive somewhere and if so did she ever think of the damage she left behind. Guilty feelings always took over the anger these questions created. Her mother was a good mother and a good wife. Why would she just leave them? If she was alive, somewhere, surely she was heartbroken too. No matter what thoughts came, she instantly discarded the ones where her mother was dead.

Mara was able to maintain some friends and some-what of a social life with GG. She was never allowed to have a boyfriend though, and never a night out past ten o'clock. She wondered if life with her father was going to be the same or if he would be a little less re-strictive. After all, she was going to live there and attend the town's high school. He had to know she was going to make friends and have some kind of social life. At least that's what she hoped.

She carefully folded the dress and placed it back into the bag. She lifted the end of her mattress and placed the bag between it and the box spring. She didn't want to risk her father finding it but for some reason she could not bear to throw it away.

That night as Mara lay in bed she recalled the excitement she felt as a small child when her mother would walk through the door and kiss her good night. Now that GG had passed away, she wondered where she was going to get womanly advice. She hoped her dad was up for the job but she was also unsure about her ability to share all her needs with him.

Mara didn't remember many kids from her first year of elementary school. Socializing away from the house had not been allowed, so her friends quit coming around once they started middle school. She wondered if she would know anyone there or if she could fit in now.

She tried to quit thinking so she could go to sleep but it was impossible. The excitement of being home mixed with the sorrow that GG was gone. Wondering what life with her dad was going to be like, a new school, making friends. It was all changing, everything in her life. There was no way she could go to sleep. She looked at the clock, 11:21. She got out of bed and walked downstairs to see if her dad was awake. The house was dark and she was alone with a hundred things running through her mind. She went back upstairs, and put on her black yoga outfit, and tennis shoes.

She slipped back downstairs and quietly left out the back door. She followed the driveway to the road and turned left to walk toward the lake in the woods where she and her mother shared time picnicking and fishing. She wanted to feel near her mother right now and talk out some of her concerns. She forgot how dark it could be in the country, but the moon illuminated her way down the road. She never tried to go to the lake at night but she was sure she could get there as long as she walked a straight line from the curve warning sign.

She knew the sign should be coming up at any time so she began to look for it. She was nearly there when a set of headlights blared into her eyes.

Chapter 2

Johnny Thomson was running late to get home before curfew. He was swearing at his parents under his breath. If they had not sent him alone on that fencing job after football practice, he would have had more time to spend with Julie. Lately it seemed his parents were finding more for him to do in the business, limiting his time for personal relationships. Now they expected him to make his curfew with no extension of time for the work he had done for them. He was going too fast when he rounded the curve, and noticed someone walking along the road, but there wasn't enough time to stop. He cringed at the thud at the front of his truck and again as he felt a thump beneath it. He stopped. His mind raced. What had he done? He reversed his truck and scrambled out.

He found Mara lying on the ground. Each time she tried to make a sound, blood gurgled in her mouth. A long gash down the side of her face bled profusely. He couldn't help noticing her eyes wide open with a fear he'd never seen and he quickly averted his eyes from hers only to see her body shaking uncontrollably. He knew she was going to die. His mind raced. 'No, no, no' it screamed. He looked around and back down at Mara. No one had seen anything. No one was around. 'Hurry, I have to hurry and get us away. Off the road, out of sight.' He placed his left hand under her neck, and reached under the crooks of her knees with his right arm to lift her Tottering in his steps, quivering in fear at the horror of what he had done, he caught himself from falling backwards. He laid her on the asphalt at the back of his truck and lowered the gate to the bed. He loaded her into the truck bed and drove. He wasn't going to be home by curfew, but this was a much bigger problem. Punishment for breaking curfew would be a breeze compared to what he could be facing.

Unsure if she was still alive or how much longer she would live in her condition, his mind raced as he drove her away from the area. The only thing he could be sure about was that his carelessness caused her death. Nothing could change that. If he took her to the hospital or to the County Sheriff's office, they would charge him with manslaughter or reckless homicide or something that would get him locked away. He wondered what in the hell she was doing out there anyway. Thoughts of his parents, school, and Julie flooded his mind and he could not face the possibility of them knowing what he'd done, he had to hide this, bury it and hope it was never found out. He turned onto a gravel road off the highway, and found a thickly wooded area and parked. The only light came from his headlights; he reached over and dropped the glove com-partment door to retrieve his flashlight. He walked to the back of the truck and lowered the gate, trying not to look into her eyes as he raised her from the bed and carried her through the trees. His adrenaline pumping so hard that he was unaware of her movements as she lowered her hand down to his pants pocket and removed his wallet.

Lying on the hard ground she could hear, almost feel his footsteps walking away. Tears of anguish streaked her face as she moaned in effort to get him to come back and help her. She thought if he could hear her, know she was alive, he would have to get her help. A light moving backward, then forward came into view.

He was returning. She thanked God as hope set in. But that hope was violently ripped from her as she lay silent, weak, and helpless listening to the whispery sound of the dirt sliding off the end of the shovel. She placed his wallet into her jacket pocket. Shattered and cold, unable to do anything, she gave in to the state of listlessness she was battling. The hole was only a few feet or so deep but he carried her far enough into the woods where he hoped she would not be found. He picked her up and placed her into the shallow grave. Desiring an end to this night-mare, he hurriedly covered her with dirt and ran back to his truck.

He tossed his shovel into the vehicle and as he lifted the gate, he saw her blood. He looked down at his clothes and saw her blood on his shirt. Frantically, he climbed into his truck and threw the flashlight into the passenger seat. He had to fix this before he could go home. He headed to town where he pulled into the Wash & Ride.

His hand shook as he deposited the coins into the slot. He lifted the sprayer from the rack on the wall and began power washing the front bumper. He walked to the back of the truck and sprayed out the bed, being careful not to clean all the dirt off its exterior. Lastly, he removed his t-shirt, hung it on the sprayer rack and washed it down. There was a spot of blood on the lower front of his left pant leg. He used one hand to scoop soapy water from a puddle as he scrubbed at it with the other.

***

Mara was jarred back to consciousness by someone or something dragging her by one of her feet. She tried to open her eyes but there was too much debris in them and it was painful. She wasn't sure whether to play dead or fight. The pain in her legs and ribs practically paralyzed her and she could taste the blood in her mouth.

The animal released her foot and smelled her from her legs to the top of her head. Its hot breath pressed her face before it began licking. She stiffened but tried to remain passive and not slap at it. She kept her eyes tightly closed, squinting until they ached so badly she could keep them closed no longer.

Darkness and moonlight created only a shadow being on four legs, but its size seemed impossible for a dog. It walked around her until the lunar light revealed it. Brilliant smoky gray eyes surrounded by a mask of silver stared into hers. Her mind reached back to a day eight years earlier. She and her father were fishing at the lake. She remembered she had become bored and gone off to chase butterflies. She saw a flash of eyes, like two small lights glowing from the edge of the woods. *Could this be the same eyes?* She looked into them again and then at the wolf as a whole. Since that day, she always felt watched by something unseen. *Had it been this creature all along, was it watching her this very night?*

It reached over and put a paw on her arm, lowered its head and nuzzled its nose against her cheek. It looked in her eyes again, turned its head away from hers and scratched her arm rough enough to break the skin. Shocked, she tried to sit up but found the pain of raising her head excruciating. She lay back on the hard earth and wondered how long she had been unconscious. She looked over at the wolf but it just sat there watching her as she worried she could be its next meal. Her injuries pre-vented any more speculation. She closed her eyes.

She was afraid to sleep in the darkness of the woods with the wolf watching her like its prey but sleep came on her anyway. She had a wonderful dream. Her head lay in her mother's lap. Her mother was stroking her hair and humming to her. Then the scene changed to Mara's dad sitting at the kitchen table, crying in anguish.

Coldness woke her and she laid there looking at the blue-gray of night becoming day before moving her fingers, her toes, then her legs, she raised her arms and rolled over on her side. The wolf rose and wagged its tail as Mara realized she only felt a little achy and she had actually rolled over.

She stood and walked a few steps from the pine needle bed before the wolf nudged her back to the ground. With eyes of fierce determination, it glared at her, and then dipped its nose towards its back. She knew it wanted her to get on and even though the animal was large enough in girth and in height, who ever heard of anyone riding a wolf. She did as the wolf wanted. She climbed up, straddled its back as best she could, and wrapped her arms around its neck. It rose from the ground and took off much quicker than she expected.

Chapter 3

Ray entered the room to find Mara's bed empty. He quickly headed downstairs calling out for her but there was no reply. Rushing outside he glanced around the porch and yard. "Mara," he yelled turning his head to the left. "Mara," he shouted turning his head to the right. He stood still there for a moment with his hands on his hips and his head down listening. *Come on baby*, he sighed, *answer back. Where are you?* Still there was no sound, no movement.

He went back into the house and hastily grabbed the phone off the wall.

"Good morning, Serenata Sheriff's Department, Sheriff Norton speaking."

"Jack, listen, it's Ray," panicked and breathing heavily he continued, "Jack, Mara's gone."

Sheriff Norton's good mood turned into a somber one, "Ray, what do you mean gone?"

"I went to her room to get her up for school and she's gone."

"Calm down Ray, I'm headed your way, just let me call Deputy Marks and get him headed over there."

"Thanks Jack, and Jack," Ray paused and took a breath, "please hurry." He hung up the phone and sat down at the kitchen table. His mind could not help going back to the day Nora went missing. He placed his head in his hands and waited for his friend.

Twenty minutes later, he answered the knock at his door. Jack grabbed and hugged him, "Ray I prayed all the way here I'd get a call from you saying Mara had shown up safe and sound."

"I don't understand this. Where could she be? She didn't sneak out with friends. She doesn't have any around here."

Ray remembered his arguments with Mara about the way he protected her after her mother's disappearance. He couldn't stand to let her out of his sight when she visited on the weekends. He was so afraid of losing her too. In time, what friends she did have slowly quit coming around or calling. He wondered now if she was afraid her life with him would be so bad.

Jack laughed nervously, this was just too surreal, that they should find themselves mulling over the disappearance of Mara. Ray's eyes flashed at him in anger, "I don't know what you think is so funny right now!"

Jack lowered his eyes and sat on the couch, "I'm sorry. I didn't mean to laugh. It's just, well, it's like a nightmare Ray. I drove here replaying our phone conversation, over, and over. This doesn't seem right to me. Are you sure she hasn't just gone for a walk. You are kinda pushing it to think she can just jump right into school today. Don't you remember how awkward and nervous we were our first day of school? And she is a teenager to-boot?"

"Well why didn't she come home when I called her? You answer me that Jack?"

"I don't know Ray. Have you looked around the house to see if there's anything suspicious?"

"No, not really. I've called out for her a few times and sat out on the porch waiting for her, for you. Whoever came first."

"Let's look around. We can't do anything else right now but look to make sure there's nothing suspicious to be found. Maybe she'll show up and we'll have worried for nothing. I'll go outside, walk the area and call her name. You check the doors and windows for signs of a break in."

Jack walked the perimeter of the house, calling out Mara's name at each corner as he went. He hoped that if she heard his voice instead of her father's, she'd realize she needed to return home. He watched closely for any disturbances in the grass and dirt that would lend as a clue to anyone standing or walking around the outside of the house. He checked the windows for scrapes or breaks and as he looked up at Mara's room from the back of the house he saw Ray looking down at him shaking his head.

Ray was running downstairs as Jack entered the front door. "I'm not seeing anything Jack."

"I didn't either and I really hoped Mara would pop out from the trees when she heard my voice." Jack said. The two men sat on the couch again, Ray with his elbows on his knees and his head in his hands. Jack leaned forward and drummed his fingers on the heavy oak coffee table as he considered the situation.

Jack looked apologetically at his friend, "I'm sorry again about the laugh Ray, I just, I don't know. This is all so crazy. I just didn't want this to be real." He got to his feet, "Right now I need you to give me a photo of Mara that is as recent as possible."

Ray walked over to the fireplace and pulled Mara's picture off the mantle. He carefully removed it from the frame and reached out to hand it to Jack. "This is Mara's school photo from last year," Ray said, looking at the picture for a moment longer before letting go of it.

"She sure turned out beautiful, got a lot of her mother in her," Jack looked at the picture and bit his lower lip in regret for having made the last comment.

"Yeah," Ray quietly agreed.

Jack didn't need to remind Ray that they'd been through this before. He used every tool at his disposal to find Nora, locally and nationally, but he had not. All he had been able to do was recover Nora's abandoned car at Ernie and Katie's cabin. Mara didn't have a car. Unless she was taken, it didn't seem likely she'd be far away.

"Ray, we're going to do everything we can," Jack reassured him, "and in this case we can start right now. Deputy Marks will be here soon and he can help you begin a search while I go to the station and release the story to the press. The sooner we get out the APB and the Amber Alert the better our chances are of finding her."

Jack shook Ray's hand and Ray thanked him, "I appreciate you working so quickly on this Jack."

"No problem, you know how much Mara means to Jenny and me."

***

As soon as Jack was inside of his cruiser, he called his wife. "Jenny, honey, I've got some bad news. Are you sitting down?"

Jenny's heart sank to her feet. When someone was worried if you were on your feet, it usually meant they were going to tell you something that could knock you down. She just wanted him to get on with it, get whatever it was, said. "Jack, please, just tell me what it is?"

"Mara is gone." Jack heard a gasp.

"Oh my God Jack! What happened? What do you mean gone?" Jenny asked.

"Ray found her bed empty this morning and she seems to be gone. Just gone." Tears formed in his eyes and he heard Jenny begin to sob.

She stepped back from the sink and leaned against the kitchen island. "I can't believe this. Please, Jack, please tell me this isn't real. Roll over and wake me up."

"Honey I wished it was that easy but this is real."

"How is Ray holding up?" Jenny asked.

"As well as can be expected. But Jenny this doesn't look well on him."

"I know. First his wife, now his daughter. People are going to talk."

"I'm afraid so," Jack agreed. "Can you meet me at the station?"

"Sure, hon. I'll be there soon."

After ending the call, Jack immediately regretted he had not delivered the news to Jenny in person. His mind was flooded with memories of the dinners they'd shared with Ray and Mara, mostly the many smiles of Mara, and the way Jenny looked at her so lovingly.

Chapter 4

Johnny was anxious to get out of the house before his parents woke up. It had been hard to focus on everything they were saying to him last night when his mind was still in the woods at that girl's grave. So many shoulda, woulda, coulda's going through his brain like a fast, passing freight train.

He rolled out of the bed and pulled his jeans up from the floor. He grabbed a clean Tee shirt out of his drawer and slipped it over his head. As he bent over to grab his boots, he noticed his jeans felt a little loose. He reached behind him and realized his wallet was missing. He slipped his boots onto his feet to dash out to the truck. He searched frantically across the dash, in the seats, he lifted the flashlight from the passenger side and checked the floorboards. He put the flashlight back into the glove box and hurried back to his room. It wasn't on the floor, on the bed, or under the bed. "Where is my damned wallet?" he whispered. He grabbed his keys off the dresser and ran back out to the truck. He had to find it before someone else did. There was no link between him and that girl and he sure didn't need his orange and white football player's wallet or his driver's license to lead back to him. He had to return to the place where he had left her.

He drove slowly as he approached the area where he struck Mara, he watched for the contrast of his brightly colored wallet to jump out at him, but nothing caught his attention.

He parked his truck near the same boulder he'd parked at the night before. He opened his door and looked around at the ground before stepping out to re-trace his steps. He studied the ground around him carefully as he walked the path through the woods toward the shallow grave. He turned to look behind him, unable to believe he was here again. Cursing under his breath, as he realized he had to see her grave again, but it could have worked its way out of his back pocket between the digging and the bending he had done. He turned quickly to look but in just a few short steps, he realized the grave was empty. Panic set in, he put his hands on his head and began pacing. He couldn't imagine how someone found her so quickly and easily. Hunting season was not open yet and he was sure there had been no headlights around. He knew he had not been followed and he knew she hadn't gotten up and left of her own accord. His wallet was not there either. He sat on the boulder unsure what he was going to do next.

This nightmare was never going to end and now with the possibility he was going to be found out, he was more afraid than ever. His heart pounded in his ears as rapidly as his mind raced. It was bad enough he'd hit her and taken her life but he'd buried her like a stray dog, to cover up his mistake.

He contemplated running, getting out of town, but with only twenty dollars in his pocket and less than a quarter of a tank of gas, he realized the idea was pointless right now. It would be another five days until his father would pay him again. He would just play it cool, pretend today was just another day. Pretend his life was the same as it had been before last night. He had to go to school and he needed to go now.

As he rounded the curve driving back to town, he passed his girlfriend's father. They nodded to each, the way people in small towns do, but it was anything but usual for Johnny. He drove looking in his rear-view mirror until the Deputy was out of his sight. He just hoped Mr. Marks wouldn't become curious about passing him in the area so early in the morning.

***

When Jack arrived at his office, he was glad to see Jenny waiting for him. "Hey Hon, can you put a copy of this photo on a regular size sheet of paper so I can get a fax ready for the press releases."

"Sure Babe." She took the photo from his hand and looked at it before laying it face down on the glass of the copy machine. It was terrible to think about Ray losing his daughter, especially the same way they lost Nora. The idea that one person could just disappear from your life and you never learned what happened was one nightmare enough but to have it happen to you again was just hell on earth. She missed the friendship she and Jack shared as a couple with Nora and Ray. Mara was the closest thing to having her own child Jenny ever experienced.

Jack called some local law enforcement offices, who said they could loan him a few men to aid in the search. He hung up the phone and began to write a brief description of Mara on the paper next to her picture. He handed it back to his wife and pointed to the fax machine as he picked up his Rolodex. She dialed the fax numbers as he rattled them off.

"Well that's it I guess. Since Mara is a teenager they won't issue the Amber Alert until she's no longer considered a runaway."

Jenny held up the fax copy, "Can I use this to make some copies for fliers? I'll call some friends and we can begin posting them around the county?"

"That'd be great," Jack brushed a blonde lock of hair and kissed her on the neck, picked his hat up from the desk and placed it on his head as he walked out the door.

Neither one of them wanted to engage in small talk or mention the searing question on their minds. Could Ray be behind all this somehow?

***

When Johnny arrived at school, he found Eddie, Val, and his girlfriend, Julie Marks, in front of the gymnasium Their conversation seemed more animated than usual. When Johnny approached the questions shot at him in rapid fire. "Have you heard about the girl here in town? She is missing this morning!" " I didn't even know we were getting a new student. Did you?" and - "What do you think happened?"

Julie smacked her gum as if she were devouring her worst enemy, "Yeah, for real, I heard my dad on the phone with Sheriff Norton. He got called in to help in the search."

Johnny grabbed Julie up into his arms and she quickly kissed him on the cheek. He raised his eyebrows and felt a slight pang at the idea of something having more importance to her than he did right now. Especially something he wanted so hard to forget. "What's up? I don't get a 'hello', just a kiss on the cheek 'cuz some crazy chick is missing?" They laughed with him as he put his arm around Julie's waist and kissed her.

"You have to admit it is kind of exciting." Julie said between chews, "Nothing ever happens around here. And she's like, our age."

"So? None of us knew her, so why should we be wasting our breath talking about it." Johnny tried to think of anything he could say to steer the conversation in a different direction.

Val cleared her throat, "I think I was in her class in elementary school. We were in the first grade together."

Eddie interrupted her, "Oh yeah, well where she's been? I don't remember ever meeting her." Eddie believed himself the Casanova of the high school, he was after all the quarterback, and he was supposed to know every girl in town.

Val replied with a bit of a shrug, "Julie said she overheard her parents telling each other that it's the same girl whose mom came up missing about ten years ago."

"Well shoot, maybe they should look at her dad. Seems kinda suspicious to me?" Johnny moved his arm from Julie's waist and placed it over her shoulders. He tugged to walk her away, "See ya'll around." He waved his hand in the air to signal their departure.

***

It seemed throughout the day he could not escape conversations about the "missing girl. He tried to behave in his normal manner, which made it easy to keep his mouth shut, because Johnny was always too cool to be concerned about things everybody else found so inter-esting. When he was asked to comment, his answer was always the same "Why aren't they looking at her dad? Mom's missing, daughter's missing, c'mon man; I hate to quote an old saying here but if it looks like a duck..."

***

Ray and Deputy Marks spent their time traipsing through the woods behind the house. Jack was clear to Marks in their conversation that he'd felt sure Mara had just gone off to spend some time alone to sort things out and prepare herself to start a new school. She could just be suffering from first day jitters, he'd explained. He seemed confident in his belief, so Marks believed that surely they would find her somewhere hiding out. But it was to no avail so they decided to widen their scope from the property to the road.

When Jack saw them, he stopped and rolled down the window. Marks leaned inward, "Nothin' yet boss."

"Well," Jack paused, "come on. We'll go back to the house and regroup. Jenny is making fliers so they can post them everywhere. The news will break on the local stations every two hours, and Maretta and Talbott counties are lending some deputies to help with the search."

They got into the car and Jack rolled up his window. He looked over his shoulder and saw the hopelessness in his friend's eyes. Ray appeared genuine in his concern and grief but there were other cases where someone's demeanor was misleading. Jack cleared his throat. He hated to consider his oldest friend could be involved in his own wife and daughter's disappearances but as a lawman he had no choice.

Marks broke the silence, "I passed Julie's beau on the way here. He was headed into town, on his way to school probably."

"You think he might be worth talking to, maybe he noticed something, maybe not?" Jack asked his Deputy. He wanted something, anything to direct his suspicion elsewhere.

"I don't know. He may have passed other vehicles on the road or something."

"I'll stop by and talk with him this evening." Jack said. "Marks you take your cruiser and head on up to the cotton gin. See if we can borrow a few men. We've got a lot of wooded area to cover."

"Yessir."

Ray sat in the backseat with his shoulders folded in and his head aimed at the floorboard. He felt as if someone had ripped his heart from his chest in the most violent way. An iron fist gripped his guts and wrenched them in such a way, he felt he'd never live through it. He prayed to God and he begged the spirit of his grandmother that she would keep her safe. He didn't want to live with the 'not knowing'. It was hard enough learning to let go of the questions he'd asked himself for years after Nora's disappearance.

As Jack drove up the drive to Ray's house he looked into his rearview mirror again, "I know it's going to be hard to do but we're going to stay here while they do some more looking around. There's still a possibility Mara will show up and I want you to be here if she does."

***

For several hours, Ray listened to Jack's radio as he received word that they'd found nothing yet and they were extending areas of the search. Jack marked the search areas with a blue highlighter on the topography map Ray printed from his computer.
"It's going to be dark soon." Ray acknowledged.
"Yes it is." Jack sighed, "I'm gonna head on over to the Thomson's before it gets too late to talk with Johnny. We'll have a lot more help tomorrow. We have to try to stay positive. Do you want to come to the house? I hate to think of you being here alone right now."
"No, no. I'll just stay here. What if Mara comes home tonight, you know. She could, I mean."
"Sure Ray, you're probably right. So I'll see you in the morning."
"Great. Take care."
"You, too." Ray closed the door and found himself alone again.

***

Johnny's dad sent him home early from work. He wanted to go by Julie's house but he knew his dad was probably testing him because he broke curfew. He knew it would be best to go home and not risk making his dad angry with him again.
He cleared his first day of trying to put last night's events behind him. He flung himself onto the couch and turned on the T.V. just in time to see the newsbreak and a picture of Mara on the screen.
"Mara Taylor is sixteen years old and was to begin classes at Serenata High School today, but when her father went to wake her this morning she was gone.

Nora Taylor, her mother and the wife of game warden, Ray Taylor, went missing ten years ago." Johnny watched as the display became a picture of Nora, "She has not been found, and in both cases there are no clues and no signs of foul play. Ray Taylor," the picture of Nora switched to one of Ray, "is an old friend of Sheriff Norton and has never been a suspect." Mara's picture reemerged, "Mara has black hair and hazel eyes, she is 5'4" tall and weighs about 110 pounds anyone seeing this girl or having any knowledge of her disappearance should contact the local Sheriff's department." A phone number was displayed under Mara's smiling face.

Johnny's mother broke his line of sight as she walked by the television, "Don't you hear that knocking at the door?" She threw her dishtowel over her shoulder and opened the door.

"I'm sorry to bother you Dee but I need to talk to Johnny."

Johnny felt his stomach hit the floor when he heard the Sheriff's voice. He sat up on the couch as his mother escorted Jack to a seat across from him. Dee sat on the couch next to her son.

Johnny looked up from the floor and sat back, crossing his legs. He had to hide his nervousness, had to be himself, cool and collected.

Jack leaned forward, "My Deputy says he noticed you up on Old Jackson Road this morning and I just need to ask you some questions Johnny."

"Yes sir, I remember passing him."

"I guess you've heard by now we have a girl missing up there?"

"Well I did hear some buzz at school and it's on T.V., but I don't know anything else."

"Did you see any other vehicles up in that area?"

"No sir. I wish I could say I had."

"You're sure?"

Johnny seemed to think for a minute, "I'm sure."

"Okay. That's all I needed to know. I appreciate your time." Jack stood up and Dee followed him to the front door. Johnny breathed a quiet sigh of relief. As Dee opened the door, Jack turned to look back at Johnny. "By the way, what were you doing up there?"

"Huh?" Johnny replied, unprepared for the sudden question, "I noticed my pole digger was missing from the back of my truck so I rode to the Bryson's to see if I'd left it there."

Johnny mentally patted himself on the back for his ability to come up with such a great excuse, and so suddenly too.

"That's right Sheriff, we did send him there alone to put the fencing poles in around their property."

"Okay. Well you folks have a good night."

"You too Sheriff and good luck, I hope ya'll find that girl real soon." Dee said.

She closed the door and sat back on the couch, she fussed with Johnny's hair for a minute. He reached up and pushed her hand away, "Mom. Stop."

"Imagine that Sheriff. Why would he even question what my boy was doing anywhere?"

Johnny tried to pretend he was still watching television as his mother went back to the kitchen. He was glad she didn't wait for an answer or try to have a conversation with him. He wasn't sure what happened to Mara's body but he was glad to know they hadn't found anything either. He prayed to God that they would never found her. He prayed to God that they never asked him about it again. The more he planned his exit strategy out of town, the more complicated it became, and he wasn't looking forward to living a life on the run. He prayed to God that it had never had happened. He prayed and he covered his silent praying with channel surfing.

Chapter 5

Ray did not go to bed nor sleep Monday night or Tuesday night. He had hoped Jack would learn something useful from his interview with Johnny but he had not and Tuesday's search was even more of a blur for him than Monday. The search team now included twenty-eight men, some from the cotton gin, some from the county co-op, and Deputies from neighboring counties. Even though they used more men in Tuesday's search and were able to cover quite a bit more of the area, they had not found any signs of Mara.

The day ended with a decision to move the search team's headquarters and starting point to another area. The most familiar place to most of the men in the county and the outlying areas was at Old Jackson Road near the Perkins Farm. It was a popular hunting place but it was also about twenty miles from his house.

Wednesday morning as he showered and changed clothes he tried to think of a way, any way Mara could be so far away on foot because the obvious conclusion, the only answer that came to mind, was unacceptable to him.

On the drive toward Perkins Farm, he noted there were more trees than he had realized. Frustration grew in him and he began to wonder why he ever wanted to live this far away from the city in the first place. Of course, the truth was, his job as Game Warden deemed it more convenient, and the state provided his home. Now, he wondered if his career choice had been worth the loss of his wife, and his daughter. He shook his head, trying to shake off his concern that the turnout this time would be the same as it had been with Nora. Surely today they would find Mara and she would be okay. They say lightning doesn't strike the same place twice, but it was beginning to feel like his case was going to be an anomaly.

Deputy Marks greeted Ray with a cup of coffee and a friendly nod of his head. He noted the look of despair on Ray's face as Ray forced a smile and nod in return. Ray accepted the cup of coffee with a slight shrug and sat down next to Jack. Jack looked up and then motioned to a Deputy from Maretta County, "Do we have an ETA on Travis and Grace?"

"Yes sir, they'll be here in about ten minutes. They want to start at the house and work from there. The point of disappearance and all."

"That makes sense." Jack looked at Ray and shook his head, "We tried everything else. We might as well try this. Grace is a good tracking dog."

They left in Jack's cruiser with Deputy Marks right behind them. When they got to the house, Jack instructed Ray to get the most recent things Mara wore.

Ray looked around Mara's room. He spied the shirt she wore her last night home. *Her last night home,* those words echoed in his mind as he ran down the stairs.

Travis took the shirt from him and pulled the hound dog's leash placing her directly in front of him. He put the shirt right up to Grace's nose and said, "Seek." Grace went out the back door, with her nose to the ground, pulling hard on the leash in Travis's hand she led him down the gravel drive to the road, where they turned left, away from town. All the search efforts prior to this had been in the woods behind their property and toward town.

Ray realized he had not considered the lake and Mara might have gone there. To admit she left and did not come home when he called out to her was just something he had not been willing to consider. Emotions of anger and concern sent him into a conflict. He turned to Marks who waited at his cruiser for further orders, "I think I may know where she went. Can you take me there?"

Marks opened the door to his car for Ray and as Ray climbed inside he said, "I think she may be at the lake."

They passed Travis, Jack and Grace but just as they arrived at the opening trail to the lake, Deputy Marks' radio piped in, it was Jack and they had found something. Marks turned the car around. They found the small search team standing just off the road around the bend.

Grace was pacing over a small area of pavement. Travis and Ray stepped out of the vehicle and walked toward Jack who soon approached them and placed his hand on Ray's chest, "Stay right here."

As Jack and Marks advanced to the area where Travis stood, Jack removed a small flashlight from his belt and aimed it toward the road to get a better look at the spot. He determined it could be blood. Marks looked over his shoulder at Ray. "Oh no Boss that's not a good sign." Julie was the same age as Mara and if anything happened to her, well he just couldn't imagine what Ray must be going through but he knew it had to be an indescribable emptiness.

Jack noticed the look on Marks face. "Don't jump to any conclusions, it could be animal blood. We'll keep searching the area, roadsides, brush, ditches and all. You notify them at the tent we've found something and need to canvas the area while we still have some daylight left."

Once he was back at his vehicle, Marks grabbed his patrol car radio and relayed the message. Within half an hour, the whole search team was covering the area. They searched from the edge of Ray's property to the edge of the neighboring property, covering a four square mile area. It was a frustrating day for many of the men as they heard about the discovery of the blood and realized how dire the situation was becoming. Many of them were already theor-izing they would never find Mara. Ray could tell which ones they were by the look of bleakness and sympathy in their eyes.

***

On Thursday, Ray was glad to see Travis and Grace waiting for them at headquarters. He tried to bear in mind that the two of them worked on some out of town cases and were successful on their searches. He was even more encouraged by Grace's eagerness as he presented Mara's shirt to her once more. She put her nose in it then lowered her head toward the ground and began to drag Travis down the road and onto a trial into the woods. She found the shallow grave quickly. She pulled Travis again, drawing him to the base of a pine tree. As they walked toward the tree, Jack noticed vehicle tracks and wanted to point them out to Deputy Marks but decided it was better not mentioning it in front of Ray. He caught up to Travis and the rest of the men. Grace walked around the tree and sat down after completing her inspection.

Everyone waited and after a few seconds Travis squatted next to her and began rubbing her neck, "I'm sorry guys but that's it."

"How can this be it?" There was a desperate edge in Jack's voice.

"The scent trail ends here." Travis stood and began walking Grace towards the car.

"But where is she? She's not here!" Ray hollered back toward them.

Jack understood the desperation Ray felt and he wanted to help him but with the evidence found, Ray's presence could create conflict in the case. The longer the search continued the more emotional Ray was becoming. It was going to be hard but he had to get Ray to stay away somehow.

"Ray I don't want to do this man, but you need to go home now and let us handle things from here.

"No. I can help. This is my daughter," he emphasized the word 'my', "Don't you under-stand?"

"I wasn't asking and I do understand. I hate this, but you have to go home and let me do my job." Jack pointed at the Maretta Deputy and moved his hand in Ray's direction. The Deputy took Ray's arm and walked him to the car.

"Marks, look at this drag mark," Jack pointed at the ground, "it leads to where the dog sat under the pine tree and then it just stops there."

"The width suggests it could have been a body. It don't look good does it boss?"

"No it doesn't, and did you see those truck marks over there? If this is where she was, then some-body came back and got her." They walked to the boulder and examined the tracks. "I see light footprints but only one set and they're not deep enough to suggest a person carrying the extra weight of a body from," Jack pointed to the pine tree, "there to here."

Deputy Marks folded his arms across his chest and put his right hand up to his mustache in contempla-tion. "I just don't know boss. I don't know what happened here. We got Grace saying she was here, and then, based on the evidence, we are supposed to believe she just disappeared into thin air. That's just crazy."

Jack swept the pine needles around the base of the tree, "There are a few shoe prints here, but they don't go anywhere. They just stop."

He and the Deputy walked the outer perimeters of the pine needle bed looking for any other clues that would lend to the story of what occurred.

Jack removed his hat and rubbed his head, "I don't know what else to do. We can have the tire tracks looked at but they're likely to match nigh on half the

trucks in this county. I don't see anything else we can
do at this juncture."

The men walked back to their cars more perplexed
than ever. Jack dreaded explaining to Ray that as
hopeful as they'd been to find an end to this ordeal,
they were left with only more questions.

Chapter 6

The last several days had been full of revelations and mixed emotions. Mara barely remembered or even recognized the cabin where the wolf abandoned her, but within its walls, she discovered the truth behind her mother's dis-appearance and, the true story behind the deaths of her Aunt Katie and Uncle Ernie. Not the stories she'd been told as a child or eavesdropped in conversations.

When she arrived, she found the back door lying against the porch, the broken windows bared shards of teeth, and growth from the forest was trying to reclaim the earth where it sat. She followed the wolf into the darkness through the broken door and walked through the kitchen. Although no one else ever lived here, the cabin was still furnished. The living room contained a chewed up rat infested couch and lazy boy both covered in dirt and rotting fabric. The tables and shelves were busted up and in disarray. Somehow, it reflected the way she felt inside, abandoned. She walked back into the kitchen. There sat an oversized butcher-block table with two long heavy wooden benches along each side of it. Bloodstains of her Aunt Katie tinged the wood just where her body had lain over the table like a child napping at its desk (that was GG's description).

Mara felt sick as the vision of that day played in her mind. She heard noises and walked back through the living room to the bedroom where they had found her Uncle Ernie, but she stopped just short of the door. She wasn't certain she was prepared to face the story the bed would tell. She'd overheard there was so much blood from the hacking of her uncle that you could not tell the bedspread had been daffodil yellow. She stood there trying to peer into the dark-ness of the room. She wrapped her arms around herself and empathized with her family's woe that prevented them from returning to this place of horrors. The wolf ran across her path and exited the cabin, a journal falling from its mouth to the floor.

Mara lifted the journal and began thumbing through it. There were entries from her Aunt but an entry from her mother caught her eye. She immediately began to read:

It is my hope someday someone will find this journal and get it to my husband, Ray Taylor or my daughter, Mara Taylor of Serenata. I hope it will give them some closure.

Ray,

I'd like to start by saying I am so sorry. When the time is right, can you please tell Mara and explain to her what happened. I love you both very much and I never intended to abandon you, but I had to know the truth.

A few months before Ernie and Katie's deaths, my sister shared a secret with me. A wolf attacked Ernie and he changed. He would go off for days at a time. I thought she was crazy. She told me wild stories about seeing his eyes blaze like fires when he got angry and he would run out of the house but by the time she got to the door, he'd be gone. I asked Ernie what she was talking about and he said I must have misunderstood her. She must have been telling me about a dream. I tried to argue with him that she was telling me this as though it was real to her but he would not hear of it.

The more I thought about their deaths, the more concerned I became and the curiosity in me was so great I had to know for myself. Ray, I would have asked you to bring me, but I know you would not have believed it and no one ever wanted to come back to my family's property again.

However, I have encountered the creature myself. It was not like the creatures of folk tales or movies from my childhood. It didn't walk on two legs but it was just as powerful and deadly.

I lured him close enough to avenge the death of my loved ones and in doing so was myself been scratched and bitten. Within hours, I changed into wolf form. My life changed forever. I would never be able to go home again. I was a threat to my family because of this curse.

I awoke a few days later and found that I was again in human form. I wanted so badly to return home but I knew I still carried the wolf in me. I cried in anguish and before I knew it, I had returned to wolf form. Once I calmed back down I was in human form. I began to realize that emotions and adrenaline are the catalysts for the change. Now that I knew this, I thought I could learn to control it. I dreamed of the day I could conquer it and be with you and Mara again, but I would have a memory or become frustrated about something and lose control. I knew it was hopeless. I just couldn't do it. I cannot return home like this. It is safer for everyone if I live my life as the thing I have become. I will have to love and watch you both from a distance. I hope you can understand now and know how truly sorry I am. I love you both so very much.

All my love,

Nora

She could not believe it. She reread the note her mother had written, especially the parts about the

wolf. It seemed just as unbelievable the second time.
What kind of craziness was this? Little Red Riding
Hood was just a fairy tale from her childhood, right?
No, this was not happening. Perhaps there was some
chance she was asleep. She pinched herself on the
arm, hopelessly, for she knew she was not dream-ing.
She remembered dreaming about her mother singing
to her and stroking her hair. That had to be a dream.
She looked at her arm, but the scratch had healed
along with the rest of her injuries. She noticed she
was in much less pain. That in itself was incredible.
She looked at the diary again, this time paying close
attention to the part about her mother's attack, and
the transformation it caused.

She had not transformed so maybe she was okay. She
laughed at herself when she suddenly realized she
must be taking this seriously to have such an idea but
this had to be some kind of a joke or a bad dream.
Then again, who would put such a story in a diary,
and why? And, wouldn't the prankster have just
mailed it to them to make sure his or her purpose was
fulfilled? But if this was a bad dream, why did it feel
so real?

She thumbed through the journal and noticed the
entries made by Aunt Katie about Uncle Ernie. She
wrote of instances where he would become angry and
run from the house, disappearing into the woods.
Her final entry was the most chilling, an entry explaining their deaths. During their last argument, he
failed to make it out of the house before his change
occurred and he attacked her.

She grabbed her cast iron skillet in defense and hit
him square on his head. He yelped and ran, busting
the kitchen window out as he escaped.

Reading on, Mara could see that Aunt Katie expressed
the same incredulous belief in this as she felt. Aunt
Katie wrote further that she waited for Uncle Ernie to
return home. He said nothing about the event but he

would not look at her either. He headed straight for the bedroom and shut the door.

Her notes concluded that she planned to wait until Uncle Ernie was asleep at which time she was going to remove his head from his body. He had one silver bullet in his hunting safe. It had been fashioned as a novelty item, a joke but it seemed the joke was on them. She noted that she was going to use it to shoot herself in the head, hoping to protect their loved ones and anyone else from the monsters they had become.

Mara closed the journal and understood the fears her mother expressed in the letter. There were so many questions in Mara's mind. Would her mother come to her? Was she going to become a wolf? Had she become a wolf already?

She went back to her mother's letter and noted the explanations that caused the change to overtake her. She decided she would put herself to the test. She had to know if she'd been affected and if she had, she had to find a way to control the situation. She didn't have to be like her mother or her Uncle Ernie.

She fell asleep on the floor with the diary in her hands.

***

A hunger she had never known awakened her and her eyes felt like orbs of fire. Muscles were twitching and contracting. Her head ached. Worst of all, she felt the urge to satisfy her hunger so strongly that she could kill right now.

She pulled her legs into her stomach as she lay on her side, the pain intense, all over. Was this it, she thought, is this what it will be like?

She could feel her face stretching out from the back of her head, tingling and pain in her gums.

Her legs felt as if they were drawing up, as her arms reached around them harder she realized her hands were no longer there. She rose up on her knees only to find herself standing on all fours, as she turned her

head to look she saw the snout at the end of her face.
No not her face she realized, a wolf's face.

She took off into the woods, her paws pounding the
ground in a hard run. Panting, the air on her tongue,
she could feel her power and the magnificence of what
she was, and she loved it.

She could smell the bark on the trees, the dirt, all the
different scents of the greenery, water, and other
animals. She could hear things, near and far, sounds
from the woods, cars from the main road miles away.
She heard tiny thump sounds, so she stood still next
to a tree and waited. A swamp rabbit made its way
near her and before she could think, it was in her
mouth. Its blood was so warm and surprisingly it
tasted good to her. She felt its rapid, little heartbeat,
and she felt the moment when its life left its body.
She dropped it on the ground and used her paws to
tear in and rip the muscles from its legs. Her jaws
salivated as she bit hard and chewed.

She walked back to the cabin with her head down and
her tail between her legs, looking back once at the
carcass of the animal she would have called cute
yesterday.

Disgusted with what she had just done she ration-
alized that it was the wolf. The idea she could be so
conscious and aware and the beast within her out of
her control made it difficult. What she'd become and
its actions led to a touch of anger with her mother.
Just as quickly as the anger happened, an apprecia-
tion that she was still alive occurred to her.

Now that her mother had saved her life and they
shared what she knew would have to remain between
the two of them, she wondered if this would give them
back their relationship. This new life her mother
gave, this had to bond them together, and if she was
not going to allow this horror to keep her from going
back home, her mother might follow. She felt she
could understand on some level why her mother had
not returned but the emotional side of her, the side of
her that grieved her mother. The child who lost her

was still in there. Confused and conflicted. The little girl who couldn't, no, would not hurt her father. She would not create that pain that never goes away because of unanswered questions and a lack of closure.

***

The day passed without the wolf returning, but Mara knew it had to be her mother and she wondered if she was a beautiful wolf also. A broken mirror pitched against the living room wall presented her the opportunity to look at herself. Two piercing, blue eyes stared back at her. There were times in her life when she looked in a mirror and seemed a stranger to herself, but this was so much more than that. This was her, another form, a hairy, four-legged wolf with pointy ears atop her head, but nonetheless her. She noticed the darkness of her gray coat and her mask of light grays and browns. On the left side, a thin bald line ran from the bottom corner of the mask toward her ear. It reminded her of the accident and a flash of anger ran through her. She saw the anger in the reflection of the wolf as its lips curled above its teeth, but there was no way this was really happening.

She ran away from the cabin quickly, she felt her strength and speed. She loved it but she knew any minute she would wake up and this dream would end. She pushed herself harder trying to wake but it wasn't helping and she found herself at the side of the highway. She hung her head and walked back into the woods, back towards the cabin.

What was wrong? Why wasn't she waking up? This was wrong on so many levels she didn't even know where to begin. Could it be that GG's death and coming home to face a new school was more than her mind was capable of dealing with at this point in her life? Maybe, being back home and dealing with all these things caused her to miss her mother even more than she realized, and it was causing her to have this bizarre dream. No. That doesn't seem right.

She arrived at the cabin still in wolf form and full of disbelief. She must have slipped into a coma in the other world or something. But, does that mean the accident really happened? And, if so could this be real too? She laughed to herself. No, this can't be real. She stretched out on the floor of the living room and went to sleep. She dreamed a dream of being at home asleep in her bed. Her mother waking her up for school and she told her mother about the wolf dream. Her mother laughed and asked, "You mean like this?" Suddenly she changed into a wolf. Startled, Mara sat up.

She watched as her arm moved and her hand rose to her face and wiped her eyes.

This has to be real. How could I have a dream in a dream and what happened to my clothes?

She stood and began looking for her clothes. She found them on the floor at the door and picked them up. They were oddly stretched and torn in some places but she put them back on and pulled the cord around her waist to keep them from falling.

She removed the wallet from the pocket of her jacket and flipped it over in her hand, studying the letters SHS embroidered on the nylon front and realized they were the initials of Serenata High School. She took the driver's license from it. A picture of a boy with soft, brown eyes beneath curly, blonde hair stared back at her. He had nice dimples to go along with his smile, too. Those dimples probably won over the girls and got him out of a lot of trouble with the women in his life. He looked almost too angelic for a guy and she was having a hard time believing as she looked at his photograph that he could do something like he did to her.

Wow. As if she weren't already nervous about attending a new school. How could she go home and go to school where he would see her? His mind would not be able to rationalize the fact that she was alive and well. How could she ever explain to him or anyone what happened that night? He tried to hide what he did *maybe he won't say anything*. There was no way for her to anticipate his reaction, so she decided not to speculate on questions she couldn't possibly answer. There were more pressing matters for her right now.

She wanted to get back home as quickly as possible. Back home to Dad. She could learn how to control this, she had to learn how to control this. She would not cause the same pain for her father that her mother had caused. She knew the strength of the wolf but she knew her human strength, her will had to be more.

She found a piece of old drapery and shook the filth from it. She tried not to think about all the bugs and vermin that used it for bedding, but she closed her eyes to protect them.

She removed her clothes and wrapped the drape around her. She walked outside and stretched a little before beginning a slow jog around the cabin. She increased her speed with each circling. Midway through her third trip, she felt her eyes begin to burn and muscles contracting. Her body lurched forward and she took off on four paws into the woods.

She slowed her pace and raised her nose taking a good breath of air into her mouth. She wanted to smell another wolf scent. Her mother hopefully but of the many smells there were, sadly her mother's scent was not one of them.

Mara tried several spots over the hours and the only luck she'd had was the vague trace of her mother around the back door of the cabin.

She sat next to the drapery and began to try the transition back into her human form.

She felt ripples of warmth wash over her body as she began to relax. The muscles in her legs and arms were letting go, releasing the tightness and she could feel them getting smaller as she noticed the tingling in her face, her jaw contracting, giving release to her teeth and sinuses. She reached over with her right hand, grabbed the curtain and pulled it around her. She rested for a few moments.

She stood and began to walk around the cabin picking up the pace as she continued her circle. This time she fought the change on the first muscle contractions by sitting on the ground and taking deep breaths. The contractions slowed down but her eyes were still burning so she imagined a beautiful, peaceful meadow with huge bright flowers in oranges and yellows and hundreds of butterflies. Everything subsided and she was ready to try again, and again, and again until she was in control.

Chapter 7

For the last several days, she had learned to face and embrace the undeniable truth. She was this thing now. A wolf, like her mother had become a long time ago.

It had robbed her father of his wife and taken their family apart as if it was nothing. The truth about Aunt Katie and Uncle Ernie had been more than her mother could stand, and when she'd become part of that truth it scared her from the life she'd known, the loved ones who needed her.

She spent most of the daylight hours learning to manage the wolf, feeling the signs of change as it took her over, and spent the evenings to hunt and feed. The shifts were more controlled and easier to manage. She would look, listen and smell the air trying to find her mother. She wondered at night as she tried to sleep why her mother was not returning now.

***

It was a challenge to find high ground and remain in the wind direction necessary to keep her scent away from the cabin as Nora watched Mara practice controlling her shifts. She hated what she had done but she loved Mara so much and she couldn't stand her life ending so soon.

What she did was wrong but she had no other alternative to save her dying daughter. Hope began to replace worry as she watched Mara learning to manage the wolf part of her. There was no doubt Mara would be able to return home. Nora's pack would not have to know what she had done, an act punishable in their pack by death. She heard tales from a family of shifters, about wolves who lived fairly normal lives among people. Her pack did not believe itself to be a species that could safely do that.

***

Mara knew she needed to return home soon. Her dad was all she had now and she was all he had. She smiled at the thought of his joy upon seeing her again. She wondered why her mother hadn't felt the same way. Why even now – now that she knew what had become of her mother – she still had not shown herself again, not even so much as left a note for her. Nothing. Still only absence.

She ran towards the woods and dropped to four paws as if it were nothing. Aware of the changes to her body as it transformed itself, accepting and letting it happen as easily as one would sit or squat. She enjoyed the power within herself but she knew these times were short lived. Once she returned home, she would have to try to ignore this side of herself and lead a normal life. She looked forward to meals at the kitchen table with her dad. Still she found eating small animals from the forest disgusting but she had to do it in order to keep her strength up. Her appetite was quite intrusive during her practices and it was in the wolf's nature to kill and eat.

Things, which had occupied her mind that fateful Sunday night – school, fitting in, boyfriends... had changed so much. She felt more confident. Coming to terms with something wild inside of her and learning to control it, had given her a strength she never knew before. Somehow, none of the rest of that stuff mattered anymore. She knew she was strong now and everything else would fall into place.

She imagined it all to be that way. She saw herself at dinner with her father. She imagined herself in class passing a note to a friend and sharing a laugh. She imagined how much better life would be so long as she let it and focused on being happy and okay with the world. Just being Mara Taylor, sixteen, daughter of Ray Taylor.

Mom was never there before, not since her disappearance. Mara would just have to be happy in the knowledge she is alive and well, even though she disagreed with the life's she has chosen – let it go now. Just let it go. She would have to dam the excitement created by the possibility she could draw her mother home, put her family back together.

The only true concern for her now was Johnny. She wondered if he had thought about her during the last week and what he'd done. Or, had he been able to bury everything about her and the events of that night. How was his life going to change when she showed up at school?

***

At three a.m., a deputy passed someone standing by the roadway. He backed up his cruiser and Mara smiled at him as he shined his flashlight in her dirty face. Amazed he threw his car into park and jumped out, "Mara? Mara Taylor?"

"Yes," she whispered.

The deputy's face lit up with a smile, "We've been looking everywhere for you for days. Your dad is gonna be so relieved. Are you okay?"

"Yeah I think so," she brushed her hair from her face and pushed up the tattered sleeves on her arms. The Deputy opened the car door and held her arm as she got inside. When he returned to his seat, he picked up the handset to his radio and requested to speak to Sheriff Norton. "Sheriff I got her and she's okay."

Norton replied and the Deputy could hear people hooting and hollering in the background, "Thank God. Why don't you carry her on down to County General Hospital and get her checked out. Ray and I will meet you up there."

"Yes sir," the Deputy put down the handset and put the car in drive.

***

The curtains opened to the examining room and Ray walked through them. He let out a cry and grabbed hold of Mara. "Honey, where have you been? What happened?"

"Daddy it's just like I explained to the Deputy. I made a stupid decision to walk to the lake in the middle of the night and I got turned around in the woods and lost my bearings. That's all Daddy and I'm so, so sorry for putting you through this." Mara began to sob and she felt a little contraction in her leg. She pulled back and asked, "Could you get me a coke. I'm real thirsty." She looked down at the floor so that her hair fell around the sides of her face to hide her burning eyes, "please."

"Sure, sure, I'll be right back," once he was gone, Mara took a deep breath to calm down. She knew she had to maintain.

Ray met the doctor at the nurse's station, "Mara's tests came back and I've looked her over really well. With the exception of what seemed to be a pretty nasty cut on the left cheek, she's fine. We'll release her as soon as she finishes her I.V. drip."

Ray sighed in relief, "Thanks Doc. Thanks." Dr. Roberts signed Mara's chart and laid it on the counter, "I'm just glad she's fine and going home Ray. I know that had to be a nightmare for you."

"Yes Doc, it really was." Ray raised the soda can a little, "She asked for this. It's okay?" The doctor nodded yes and walked toward another set of curtains.

With a big smile on his face Ray delivered the soda and the good news to Mara, "We get to go home as soon as you finish your drip. Doc Roberts already signed your release."

Mara smiled, "Home. My bed. Ah, that sounds so sweet."

***

When they arrived at the house Mara immediately went to the bathroom, her hair was a mess and she felt the heaviness of the dirt suffocating her skin. She climbed into the steaming shower and when she was done she felt brand new and ready for a good, long rest. She went downstairs and kissed her dad on the cheek, "I think I'll just go to bed for a while. I'm really tired. I love you and I really am sorry Dad." Ray hugged her neck and kissed her on her forehead, "Do you mind if I tuck you in?"

She laughed, "No. That'd be nice."

He pulled the covers up folding the sheet over the top of the blanket and she laid her arms across it. "Dad, do you still miss Mom?"

"Mara, we've been through all this before. It was settled and you understood. Your mom is gone baby and as hard as we tried we couldn't find her and after all this time I'm pretty sure she's not just gonna walk through that door."

"I know Dad, but what if?"

"Then I'd give her the biggest bear hug I could muster. I'd tell her how much I love her and missed her and then I'd spank her bottom."The image of that, made Mara laugh. "But Mara you've got to know deep down just like I do, if your mom could be here she would."

"Yeah, I guess." Mara replied quietly and her dad kissed her on the forehead just as her mother had done.

***

Mara awoke in the middle of the night, she listened to the sounds of the house and she could hear her dad's breathing as he slept. She got undressed and slipped into her bathrobe. Once she was outside, she removed it and took off running across the back of the yard and into the woods.

Her forehead, jaws and nose began to feel compressed and pulled forward. She could feel her muscles contracting, stretching and strengthening as they grew and she fell forward landing on her front paws. Almost as quickly as the change occurred, the sensations subsided. She was a powerful animal running at speeds unimaginable to her before.

She stopped for a moment to smell the air and listen. There was a faint scent of her mother and she followed it slowly so she wouldn't lose it. But when she got to the creek the scent was gone. Mara wasn't sure how long she'd been away from the house and she did not want to chance her dad waking to find her gone. There would be other nights and she wasn't going to give up. Now that she knew her mother was out there and they shared this secret, it was more important than ever to Mara to see her.

Chapter 8

The black '67 fastback Mustang sat in the driveway and he was elated about passing it on to her. He'd pulled it out of the barn that morning and cleaned it up real nice. He knew Mara would be thrilled to get it and he couldn't wait to see the look on her face. He'd waited a lot of years for this day. He ran up the steps and through the front door shouting, "Mara get out of that bed and get on down here. I need to show you something."

She grunted under her breath but she really had spent too much time sleeping and hanging out in her room. She answered back, "be there in a minute."

Her father stood at the bottom of the stairs with a huge grin on his face and a kitchen towel in his right hand, "Now wait just a minute, I need to blind fold you right quick."

She had never seen him being silly like this, but whatever, she turned and he put the towel over her eyes and tied it around her head. He grabbed her by an elbow, "Just follow my lead out the front door."

"Okay...?" she said inquisitively.

Once outside he raised the hand of the arm he'd been holding and placed a set of keys into it, then he pulled the blindfold off her head. "Oh my God, Dad, this is so awesome!" She squealed and hugged his neck

harder than she ever hugged him before, "I can't
believe it! Mom's car? You've had it all this time?"
"Yeah. I kept it in the barn and tinkered with it some
over the years as a hobby and I knew the day would
come when I would pass it on to you."
"I'm so happy. I mean I do miss GG but dad I'm so
glad to be back home, back with you. And this, Dad, I
never dreamt this would ever happen! That you'd
have Mom's car and you would give it to me."
"Well there will be rules young lady," he said sternly.
"Duh, of course," Mara groaned as she opened the car
door and sat in the driver's seat. She looked up at him
with an even bigger smile on her face, "Thanks Dad."
"You ready to learn to drive?"
"Now? Are you for real?"
"I sure am."
"I've been ready for this like, forever!"
He opened the driver's side door, "Get on in then."
She sat behind the wheel and admired the pristine
condition of the interior as he walked around and got
in the passenger seat.
"Let's see those keys." He began explaining the
function of each one, "This one goes to the ignition
and that one is for the trunk and the glove box. Now
go ahead and put the key in the ignition there," he
pointed, "and turn it to the right with your foot just
slightly on the right side pedal down there by your
foot, oh, and the pedal on the left I should point out is
your brake pedal." He couldn't believe he nearly
forgot to point that out. This was like watching her
take her first steps as a toddler but putting her behind
the wheel of a car was much more serious and he
needed to make sure he taught her well. He had to
tame his excitement for sharing this mile marker in
her life and focus on giving her better instruction.
He cleared his throat, "Just slightly press that right
side pedal as you turn the key."She looked down at
the floorboard and raised her right foot to just above

the pedal and with her hand a bit unsteady, she turned the key and pressed her right foot down ever so slightly.

The car roared to life and she felt something change in her, a sense of more independence, of more control of her destiny. She leaned back in the seat, closed her eyes and took a deep breath,

Her dad continued, "That right pedal there, that's your gas pedal and it controls your speed. The harder you push it the faster you're gonna go. So you'll want to start out pretty easy on that."

"Okay."

She listened as her father instructed her on the park, reverse and drive. When he was done, she followed his guidance in maneuvering the vehicle around the yard until the moment he decided she was ready to head down the driveway and turn onto the actual road.

For the first ten minutes, they rode in silence, he watching the road as she looked down the road to what her future could hold now that she had a car.

"You're doing so good, Mara. I'm thinking you must have natural talent for driving."

"Really Dad?" she said incredulously, "Is there such a thing?"

"Sure there is. Why do you think people choose to drive for a living? It's like second nature."

She was enjoying driving so thoroughly, she could only agree, "Yeah. I guess you're right."

"There's a driver's manual in here," he pushed the button on the glove compartment door and it dropped, "you study that tonight. We'll drive some more this weekend and if you'd like we'll get your license Monday."

"Wow. That soon?" She immediately regretted questioning him.

"I know, I'm just as shocked as you, but yeah, I think you can handle it. You're doing so well already."

Once they reached the edge of town, Ray had Mara turn around in the corner gas station so they could drive back to the house. She handled the car with caution as she turned left, back onto the road and that further instilled his confidence in her.

"You did that very well."

"Thanks Dad."

"Mara I want to talk to you about what happened last week."

"Dad it was nothing. Can't we just forget about it? I mean I've already said I'm sorry. I did a stupid thing. I know it."

"No, I don't mean." He stopped himself; it was not his intention to upset her. They were having such a good day and he didn't want to ruin it. "I want to talk to you about us I mean. About – I just want to tell you that while you were gone I thought about a lot of things."

Mara heard a tenderness in her dad's voice she never heard before, "Dad, I feel so bad for putting you through that, especially after what happened with Mom and all. I guess you could say that's what drove me so hard to find my way out and back home. All I could think about was you. What you must have been going through."

"Yeah, that incident with your mother has controlled a lot of your life. A lot in our relationship actually." He paused, "That's what I want to talk about. I was afraid I had run you off. That you didn't want to be with me, because I had restricted you from so many things in life when you were with me on the weekends. I hoped I would have the chance to make things different for us."

"I did hate that, but Dad I would never run away." Moisture formed in her eyes and she blinked away the blur it caused. "I lost my friends here and I know you tried to make my visits as nice as possible with Aunt Jenny and Uncle Jack but there was nothing else here for me to come back to. And a new school right now. I don't know anybody anymore and I'm a little freaked out."

"I know," he said softly, "but I'm sure you'll make a lot of friends pretty quickly."

She took her eyes off the road for the first time to look over at him and smile, "I love you Dad."

"I love you too, sweetie."

He handed her the driver's manual once they arrived back home and she carried it up to her room eager to learn it so that she would be able to pass her written test.

Chapter 9

When he entered her room the next morning to wake her, he grinned as he noticed the book still in her hand as she slept.

"Wake up. Got some cinnamon toast downstairs just for you."

She stretched and sat up, "I'll be down in a sec."

"I'm waiting on you."

She stopped him just as he got to the door, "Dad do you think we could listen to the radio while I drive?"

He laughed, "Sure. Maybe today we can stay away from heavy conversation, huh?"

"Yeah, as long as we don't have to debate music styles or radio stations."

"I'll try to behave." He assured her.

They ate quickly and Ray quizzed Mara from the driver's manual. She answered his questions remarkably well, with a few exceptions he marked so she could study them more carefully.

Their morning drive was more relaxed than the drive the day before when they had both been excited and nervous.

***

When Jenny arrived to pick up Mara at three that afternoon, she found her on the porch swing studying for the driver's test. "You ready to take some time away from studying?"

"Why, what's up?"

"Your dad called and said he thought you could use some girl time."

"I'd love that actually." Mara threw her legs over the side of the swing and stood up. "What are we gonna do?"

"We can go into town and eat some lunch for starters. Have you had lunch?" She asked, suddenly remembering it might be kind of late in the day for that. Before Mara could answer she continued, "Then we could go shopping, get you some new clothes for school."

"Okay Aunt Jenny, that all sounds marvelous to me." She opened the door for Jenny then followed her into the kitchen. "I'll just go let Dad know you're here and what we're doing."

"Alright." Jenny sat at the table and waited as Mara ran to her dad's study. She could hear the excitement in Mara's voice and she listened as Mara's feet pattered up the stairs to her room.

Ray walked into the kitchen with his wallet in his hand. He removed a credit card and handed it to Jenny. "Thanks Jen, I know this will be a good thing for her, so you girls have a good time.'

"I'm glad to do it Ray. I sure do love that little girl."

"I know you do." The glowing anticipation on her face made it clear and he was grateful to have Jenny be part of Mara's life.

"Look, take her to the phone center for me? If she's going to be driving to and from school I want her to have a way to reach me if she has a problem."

"That's a good idea."

Mara skipped to the kitchen, "Ready." She sing-songed.

"So Mara, you up for pizza or would you like something else?" Jenny inquired as she buckled her seat belt.

"No. Pizza is fine."

Mara played with her bracelet for a few minutes while
Jenny tried to find another topic for conversation,
"Hey why don't you find a radio station you like."
"Okay," Mara reached over and began to push the
buttons but all the programmed stations played
country music so she began to rotate the dial until she
found a rock station.
"Are you looking forward to school tomorrow?"
"I guess. I'm just a little concerned about whether I
can fit in. But Dad gave me the Mustang and that
should help."
"You'll fit in just fine Mara. You are a beautiful girl. I
don't know how you could be worried about that. Car
or no car, girls are going to be hanging on to their
boyfriends a little tighter when you show up."
"I guess. So long as I don't become the butt of a joke
about 'how does one get lost in the woods? Follow
Mara."
Jenny laughed, "Oh honey, I'm sorry, I'm not laugh-
ing at you. It's just that I don't think you have to
worry about that. You really are too pretty and sweet
for people to pick on. I think they'll be anxious to get
to know you."
"I hope you're right Aunt Jenny."
Mara looked around at the quaint little shops in the
town square, and saw a few places to check another
time. Once inside Pia's Pizzeria, they ordered the
salads and a small sausage, onion, and mushroom
pizza, recommended as the "best pizza in the joint."
After making their salads, they picked a booth next to
a picture window with a view of the town square.
"Mara, do you like being back here? I mean, you
know, at home with your dad?"
"Yeah. I'm really glad to be home with Dad but I'm
afraid he is gonna watch me like a controlling
boyfriend now."
"Well he has some honest insecurities and he loves
you very much. Last week was quite a scare for him."
"I know I still can't believe how stupid I was." Mara
reflected on last week. It was a mixed blessing but she

couldn't tell anyone about her discovery. "We talked about it some yesterday and I just hope I made him feel better. You know? About how I would never run away and about Mom."

Jenny reached in her purse and withdrew a five-dollar bill from it, which she passed across the booth to Mara, "Why don't you play something upbeat to listen to while we eat."

"Any requests?"

"Whatever you want to play will be fine with me. I like all kinds of music so it really won't matter."

The jukebox had more country music than anything but there were some 70's songs so Mara played the ones she knew. She just couldn't deal with country. Heartbreaks, hangovers and romance were not relative to her life at this point but she hoped her life was getting ready to turn a corner now that she was home.

She was ready for a social life, a boyfriend and all the things forbidden when she lived in Claramay with GG. She watched the waitress walk by with the pizza, followed her to the table, and sat down.

"Mmm, it sure smells good."

"They do make the best pizza I have ever had," Jenny reached over and removed a slice, "and it's served fresh out of the oven. Be careful it's very hot."

Mara could tell by the mozzarella strands stretching from the slice to the pan that it was definitely hot. She carefully removed a piece, placed it on her plate and began cutting it into smaller pieces so it would cool down quicker. She had not had a pizza in months. Her grandmother frowned on eating out and she'd once told Mara pizza was one of the un-healthiest foods a person could put in their body. Mara considered the fresh vegetables, tomato sauce and meat and wondered how that was possible.

Jenny finished her meal in silence, relishing the pleasure of her dinner companion's face as Mara savored the pizza.

After she wiped her mouth and laid her napkin in her plate, Jenny picked up her purse and rose from the table, "And now we move on to our next destination."
"Where's that?" Mara asked as she stood.
"Your dad gave me his card so that we can get you a cell phone."
Mara's eyes widened, "Aunt Jenny, what's Dad gonna do for my birthday when it rolls around? I mean after this weekend, I don't know what's left for him to give me."
Jenny tried to contain her giggle, "I'm sure you'll come up with something by then."
Once they left the store with her new phone in hand, she text her dad, "Thanks Dad. Love you so much."
He text right back with, "☺ - YW – Love u too."
They entered a boutique, four shops down from the phone center and began shopping for clothes. They definitely had varying tastes. Jenny would pick up a flowery top and talk about how absolutely beautiful it was and Mara would smile and think to herself, *yeah right, if you wanna draw attention to yourself by looking like a human flower pot.* But they had a great time and she found a few pair of jeans and some hoodies she really liked. Mara wondered if shopping with her mom would have been the same or if they would have had similar tastes. She wanted to believe she would eventually get to experience it.

Chapter 10

Johnny's grades were slipping and he really needed to ace this test but since the accident, his mind could not quit playing images of Mara dying. He wondered how long that night was going to continue playing itself over and over. How long would the daymares and nightmares continue before Sheriff Norton came to get him and charge him with murder? He'd been relieved the night he was questioned had gone so well. Thank God his mother was there to back up his story.

Several days passed since that night and although he had been too busy working to watch or listen to any news over the weekend, the last he heard they still had found nothing. He'd been afraid to ask Julie if she knew anything because he didn't want her to wonder why he'd be interested. He took a deep breath and slouched down in his desk, trying to relax and focus on Algebra.

There was a knock at the classroom door and Mr. Grant got up and answered it. His hand disappeared into the hall and reappeared with papers in it. He stepped back from the door to allow Mara into the room.

Johnny's hand trembled causing his pencil to drop to the floor. *No way*, he reached up and put his hand over his eyes rubbing them as if he would see someone else when he looked back at the front of the class.

Mr. Grant cleared his throat, "Class, we have a new student. I'm sure her name will be familiar to most of you, it is Mara Taylor. Let's make her feel welcome and please, please refrain from asking her questions about stories you've heard on the news."

Mara noticed the familiar scent of the wallet with a blend of fear mixed in its essence. Somewhere in this room sat the boy who hit her, buried her and left her for dead. She took a deep relaxing breath to slow down her heart rate and shove her feelings away. This was not the time to let loose the wolf. She lowered her eyes and slowly walked to her seat. She could feel his stares and sense his disbelief.

Surely, his eyes were playing tricks on him. How could he focus on equations now? He was only capable of seeing flashes of the dying girl, dead girl, buried girl and how it was impossible to equate those visions with the vision of that same girl sitting three desks over and one row in front of him. She sat there, clean, breathing, living, reading like nothing ever happened, and she never even looked at him. This was insane. He wanted to imagine it had all been a horrible dream, but as she lifted her hair over her left ear, Johnny saw the scar he had caused and knew it was her.

***

Johnny was near breakdown level by the time lunch rolled around. He sat in the cafeteria trying to control his knee bouncing. He took deep breaths and tried closing his eyes only to find that it intensified the roar in the room. It seemed to be taking forever for Julie to get to him but finally he heard the laughter of his girlfriend as she approached with their friends. He didn't mean to do it but he shot Mara a look of anger before he stopped to consider his demeanor. He knew it was a mistake as soon as he let it happen. How was he supposed to seem nonchalant about this girl's situation if he was so obviously irritated about her being found? Stupid, stupid, stupid, a voice in his head screamed.

"What's your problem?" Julie asked as she leaned in towards him.

"Sorry. I'm just upset with Mr. Turner. He said if I didn't ace my English test this Friday my grade in his class would slip to a D and I would be benched until I brought it back up. He didn't want to hear about how much I've been working and between that and practice I didn't have time to do that stupid essay on Chaucer." Johnny gave himself a mental high five for his impromptu excuse. Everyone knew how important it was to him to be in control on the field and how upset it would make him to sit out for even one game.

"Oh." Julie replied, not knowing what to say about that, but understanding.

Val reached over and gave Johnny a slight push to his shoulder, "Why didn't you tell me about the essay? I would have written it for you."

"Nah," Johnny replied with a smile. "I wouldn't want you to take your time to do that. You and Eddie have your thing going on and I don't want to butt in on my best friends time with his girl." He grinned at Eddie so hard, his nervousness nearly made him laugh, "Besides I kinda forgot about it anyway."

Quickly he got to the subject he wanted to talk about the most, as if he were just changing the subject. "So they found the new girl? Why didn't you tell me Julie?"

"I didn't think it mattered to you. I mean come on Johnny you acted like you were so over it the day it happened anyway. So why would I even think you cared one way or the other?"

"I was just curious is all." Johnny took a cherry tomato from Julie's salad. She popped the back of his hand, "Hey, get your own."

It lightened the mood around the table and allowed Johnny the opportunity to get back to his act of everything is normal.

***

Val spotted Mara looking through the reference section in the library. She walked over beside her and pulled a book at random from a shelf. "Do you remember me," she asked Mara quietly. Mara looked up from the book she was studying and recognized the girl from the same table Johnny sat at in the cafeteria. "Well you look a little familiar but I don't really remember, no. What's your name?"

"Val Kelley. We were in Mrs. Jones class together." Mara looked at her for a minute and said, "Oh yeah, you always sat in the front of the class. I was always amazed at how outspoken you were?"

"Yeah well, a quiet mouse doesn't get the cheese, right?" Val smiled, unsure about Mara's impression of her. "I guess not," replied Mara, who theorized it best to be a quiet mouse because then no one noticed you and put out the traps

"Look," Val began to write on a small piece of purple notepaper, "here's my number. You call me and we'll hang out. I have lots of free time right now. My crew is busy with football and cheerleading practice. Julie has to do some kind of fundraiser afterwards. If you like, we could spend some time together. I mean, if you want? You know do a movie or something?"

Mara politely took the piece of paper and put it in her back pocket.

The bell rang, saving her from further conversation, "Well gotta go. Dad'll be watching for me. Things are a bit tight at home right now."

"No kidding that was crazy last week for you. I heard you were lost in the woods. That must have been scary and especially after the first few days? I couldn't imagine trying to survive out there."

"Oh great! Now everybody knows?" Mara's face flushed. She tried to lay out the events the same as the lies she had told her dad and law enforce-ment. Hoping she didn't seem stupid or as fake as she felt right now, "It's been a long time since I went to the lake by the house and I got turned around." Mara laughed, trying to make light of the difficulties she had been through, "How silly was I?"

"Well at least you're alright."

"Thanks," Mara picked her backpack up and waved bye to Val as she hurried out of the library.

Mara exited the school building quickly, eyes rifling in search of Ray's truck. Once she spotted it, she picked her pace up again until she was in the safety of its cab. Ray watched as she secured her seatbelt, "Hey. How was your first day?"

"My first day at school," Mara looked up at the ceiling, "let's see... it was nice, I guess. At least as far as first days anywhere goes. I met some people and I think I may have made a friend."

"So who's this possible new friend?" Ray reached over and turned his radio down to give his daughter his full attention.

"Val, she dates the quarterback of the football team, Eddie, and they hang out with Julie, the Captain of the cheerleader's squad and her boyfriend Johnny, another football player. Anyway Val gave me her phone number and asked me to give her a call sometime."

"Well good and you were so worried about fitting in. You've already met the cream of the crop at the school. Julie is Deputy Marks daughter. Did they tell you that?"

"Dad, I really don't think that was pertinent information for their social circle. But that does explain how the kids at school know about what happened to me."

She tapped her books with her knuckles. "I can't believe all the make-up work I have. You think a girl lost for a week in the woods could get some sort of science and health credits, but nooooo."

"I guess you'll have a little more tomorrow since you missed your morning classes to get your license."

"Yeah, I didn't think about that. Oh well a kid's gotta do what a kid's gotta do." She sighed.

"Especially my kid." He stated emphatically.

***

Once she was in her room, she took Val's number out of her pocket and pinned it to the bulletin board in her room. Val seemed like a very friendly girl and she was in Johnny's group. Mara hated the idea of using her but a relationship with Val could give her an inside tract to Johnny. She and Johnny needed to talk and reach an agreement to keep their ill-fated night a secret.

Chapter 11

At lunch, Julie watched as Val approached Mara and pointed towards her. Julie raised her hand to her mouth and talked behind it at Johnny and Eddie, "Oh no you guys, she's inviting that girl over here."

"No way," Eddie gasped.

Johnny looked down at his plate and began to bounce his leg, "Maybe she won't accept, but if she does," his voice volume dropped, "I guess we'll have to deal with it and have a talk with Val later."

Julie continued watching, "Okay, here comes Val and Mara's not with her." Julie smiled at Val as she neared the table, "Is she coming?"

"No. She said she promised Renee and Shelly she was going to sit with them. Val took her seat next to Eddie and looked at her friends' blank faces. She's gonna call me after school though, we're gonna go to Dazzling Digits and get our nails done." Val added the last part as an explanation that inviting Mara over had not been a total waste of her time.

Johnny sighed and smiled at Julie, which Julie took as a signal to begin the lecture of "the Elite" with her. "I can't believe you invited her over here. I like our little group just fine and you don't even know if she'd fit in with us. I swear Val sometimes you are just too friendly. Besides there's a picture here I think you're missing – boyfriend, girlfriend and boyfriend,

girlfriend. Where does she belong in this equation?"
Julie rolled her fork around in her food, because that's
all she did after a few bites.
"Just trying to be friendly and get to know her. I don't
see anything wrong with that." Val shot back.
"Anyway you guys don't have to worry about me
trying to bring her into our group. I can just hang out
with her while ya'll are at practices. After all I can be
friends with anyone I like, right?"
"Of course you can babe," Eddie took her hand into
his but his eyes were on Julie.
"Thanks babe." She squeezed his hand drawing his
attention back to her.
"Well we really don't know her but her family has
gone through some pretty weird circumstances and
you should really be careful who you are friendly
with. Just saying."
Val hated when Julie used that phrase. It was like
an "I told you so" before whatever actual event she
imagined occurred.
Johnny saw Julie's last comment as an open door to
find out why no one had come for him yet, "Did she
say anything about where she was last week?"
"Yea. She says she just got turned around in the
woods during the night."
Johnny stared at his plate for a minute in disbelief.
He wondered what was going to happen next. What
was her motive for not telling the truth? Most of all
he wondered how she was even alive?

***

As soon as the bell rang, Val rushed to put her books
away and look for Mara. She was surprised to learn
that Mara's locker was right next to hers.
"Whoa, this is so cool. I thought I would have to look
for you." She was nearly breathless.
Mara swapped out a few books and closed her

locker. "Slow down." She turned and placed a hand on Val's shoulder, "I know the concept of CPR but I'm not sure if I could use it."

"I think you are CPR. You have no idea how much I need a friend outside of my circle. You are reviving my idle - bench spectator -filled life."

Mara continued talking as they walked to the car, "Why haven't you become a cheerleader or something?"

Val shrugged, "Julie tried to talk me into trying out this year. I don't know. I guess it's just not my thing."

Mara knew what she meant and as she put on her seat belt, she made an effort to secure her friendship. "I can understand that. Cheerleaders seem to have so much confidence in themselves." Mara had never felt that in herself, so she never felt like she could become part of that group either.

"I just don't fit that mold and if anyone knows me almost as well as I know myself, it should be her."

"So you two must have become friends in elementary school?"

"Yeah, but I remember you. You had to go live with a relative or something?" Val paused before posing the next question, "They never found your mother did they?"

"No. They didn't. My father sent me to live with his grandmother."

"Hey, if you don't want to talk about it, that's okay."

"There isn't really much to say about it. My mother went missing. She was never found. My life after that was pretty uneventful. I lived the life of an old maid under the watchful eyes of my GG."

"I'm sorry." Val looked at the floorboard. "I shouldn't have brought it up."

"It's okay. I'm sorry I bit your head off." Mara parked the car in the space marked at the curb. "It's just past and I want to leave it there." She removed her keys from the ignition and put her purse over her shoulder, and continued their previous conversation. "Maybe Julie just wanted you to be involved in her interests.

You know so you guys would be hanging out together all the time."

"Maybe so, but as you said, those things are her interest" Val replied as she opened the door of Dazzling Digits, "I just can't see me trying to be like her."

They stopped at the counter and selected the services they wanted and moved to the nail polish shelves, "Besides I wouldn't be here with you and so far I think we may have more in common and I'm glad I'm here." Mara began to feel a warming toward Val and a realization. They may truly understand each other more than she'd expected. It was just yesterday when she considered Val as just a tool to find out what was going on with Johnny. Now she had to see the possibility of this relationship becoming a friendship. They were led over to the tables to begin the application of their nails and as she sat there having her nails filed and prepped she reminisced about her friends in Claramay. She never would have used them. But she had no choice now, Val was the only way she knew for peering into Johnny's world.

They were sitting next to each other at the nail dryers when Julie walked in. She smiled and asked how they were as she passed them without waiting for a reply."

"Look at her," Mara said, "she is so beautiful and her hair is perfect all the time. How does she do that?"

"She wears those expensive hair pieces. I mean all she has to do is brush her hair, pin it up, insert a comb with a hair-piece on it and voila, she's got great hair. I wish my hair was all one length and straight so I could do that. But, whatever, I mean who's got the quarterback boyfriend?" She laughed a little laugh.

"When Eddie asked me out the first time I was kinda shocked," Val looked at the nails of her right hand, "but I really wanted to go out with him. I mean hey, he may not be the cutest boy in school but he is the quarterback. At first I was worried Eddie was just interested in me because I was Julie's friend and he was trying to get close to her but everything we did for a few weeks was all about the two of us. He hardly asked about Julie and when he did, it was about Julie and Johnny. So I knew it was me that he liked." Val smiled a grin of satisfaction.

"I saw the looks on their faces this afternoon when you were talking to me. I hope I don't create any problems between ya'll."

"No, I'm a big girl. I can hang out with whomever I want. Besides Eddie's okay with it and he's the only one that really matters to me."

"So Julie and Johnny don't like it then?" Mara studied her nails as though they were more important than Val's response.

"Julie's just different about people. I don't want to call my friend a social snob," Val scrunched her face a bit, "but she is and Johnny, he just goes along with everything Julie says."

"So he just agreed, huh?" Mara gently pressed a nail, checking to see if it was dry, "He didn't have his own opinion or anything?"

"No. He hardly ever does."

Mara's nails were dry and she noted to herself that Julie being here meant football practice was probably over, "Ya know if you'd like to run by and see Eddie before I take you home, I wouldn't mind."

"Really? I would love that. Thanks Mara."

"Sure. You know where they're working, right?"

"Yep, they're at the Jaspers'. Their daughter Celia is President of the Physics Club and her parents are having a privacy fence put up for the pool."

"Okay, we'll go by there," she stood up and flashed her hands out, "Mine are dry. How's yours?"

Val gently touched a nail, "All done."

They waved bye to Julie and she watched as they got into Mara's car and drove off.

***

"Go up here and take a right."

Mara followed Val's directions until they arrived at the home of Celia. They saw Eddie and Johnny putting the frames up for the fence sections. Val and Mara got out of the car, "I'll just wait here by the car for ya." Mara said, not sure she was ready to be in such close proximity to Johnny. He was cute, she couldn't deny it but she wondered if he was smart enough to keep what happened to himself.

Johnny froze in his posture as if he forgot what he was doing, as if nothing existed but himself and the girl he could not take his eyes from. Mara could smell his fear so strongly that it created a coppery taste in her mouth. She could hear his heart racing. He barely heard Eddie call his name and when he did, he jumped.

"C'mon Johnny. You got a girl. You wanna be on this job forever?"

"No man, I don't and this staring thing, it's not what you think."

"Yeah," Eddie laughed, "Sure it's not."

***

Mara carried Val home and went back by the Jasper's. She pulled around the corner and watched the two boys working and when they loaded the truck and left, she followed them, ducking behind a parked car on the side of the street a few times to keep from drawing his attention to her. She drove by as he pulled into a driveway. The sign in the yard read, 'Thomson Fence Co." same as the side doors of Johnny's truck leading her to believe it was his house. She parked at the corner and watched in her review mirror as they unloaded fence wire coils from the bed and she questioned herself for the reason she'd come here. She wanted to talk to him. To ask him about that night and to assure him she would not say anything if he wouldn't tell anyone anything. After all, they both had a secret to keep.

She imagined the conversation they would have and how unbelievable all this was for her. She could hear him scoff at her explanation for being well, for being alive for that matter. She imagined all the questions he would ask. Would he ask her to give him the gift if he did believe her. She couldn't do that. She looked back over at the house and noticed the truck was gone.

Chapter 12

"Hey girl, come over here," Jenny hugged Mara tightly and handed her a head of lettuce, "give me a hand."
Ray smirked, "Watch out for those nails, you got a lot of time invested there."
Jenny picked up Mara's free hand, "Those are beautiful Mara. When did you get those done?"
"Yesterday. I made a friend at school and she and I went together."
"What's this new friend's name?" Jenny asked as the men quietly excused themselves to go out and tend the grill.
"Val Kelley."
"I'm glad to hear that. This doesn't mean I've been replaced does it 'cause I'm just about ready for another girl's day out." Jenny looked up from the tomatoes she was slicing, "You up for it?"
"I'd like that." Mara began cutting the lettuce and putting it in the colander. Jenny removed the meatloaf from the oven. They set the table and Mara slid the patio door open, "Dinner's on the table."
The men joined them, and once the food made it around and their plates were full, Mara's cell phone chimed. It was a text from Val,

'Eddie not coming again tonight'

Mara text back, ''sup with that'

Val – 'don't know smthng to do w Johnny again'

Mara – 'Val ss'

Val – 'not your fault'

Mara – 'I just hate it for u'

Val – 'tysm Im thinking its petty on my part'

Mara –'I don't think so'

Val – 'talk to u tmrw'

Mara – 'sure thing'

Ray looked up and raised his brows, "Mara please turn that thing off."

"Sorry Dad." Mara held the power button down until her phone shut off. "That was Val, she's upset with Eddie and she just needed to vent I guess."

Ray swallowed the food in his mouth, "It's just poor manners to be on your phone at the dinner table. I know you have a social life now but we are company."

"I know Dad. I'm sorry." Mara mentally kicked herself because she did know better, she just didn't think about it.

"What's she upset about?" Jenny asked.

"Eddie is spending a lot of time with Johnny and leaving Val up in the air."

"Sometimes guys just like to spend time with each other. There's nothing wrong with that." Jack said, "I remember when your dad and I were in high school. We were nearly inseparable."

This sent Ray for a small walk down memory lane and he chuckled, "Yeah, we did some pretty mischievous things we never would've done with our girlfriends around. They're probably just blowing off some steam right now."

Mara knew there was more to it. She proceeded carefully, "I think there's more to it."

"Why do you think that?" Jenny asked.

"It's like Johnny doesn't want to be alone. But the way Val explained things to me, he and Julie should literally be joined at their heads. So I just don't understand why he has this thing with Eddie all of a sudden."

Ray laid his fork on his plate, "You know Mara, there are some things guys will share with each other, they would never share with their girlfriends."

"What kind of things?"

"Just things," Ray answered as if he was afraid of crossing some guy-code.

Jenny laughed, "Guys aren't really as different from us as they'd like to believe. The few things that are different usually just have to deal with," Jenny cut herself off suddenly and carefully considered her next words. She didn't want to offend the sensibilities of the men at the table but she wasn't sure how to finish her answer without doing just that, "well, let's just say they don't like to show any vulnerabilities they may have, especially in front of a girl."

"Vulnerability?" Mara asked. "You mean like fear?"

Jenny looked at Jack and Ray. She cleared her throat, "Yes, I guess that would be one of them."

Mara could understand Johnny being fearful right now. "Do you think he'd tell Eddie what's going on with him?"

Jack and Ray shared a glance, "I guess it depends on what it is." Ray answered.

"Can you think of anything at school that's going on with Johnny?" Jack asked.

"No." Mara seemed to think. She shrugged, "Nothing I've seen."

Jenny rose from the table and began to clear the dishes, "Enough of this. I'm sure Johnny can work out his own problem." She looked at her husband, "I see the cop in you trying to go to work. Relax. I'm sure it's just teen angst."

"You're probably right." Jack got up and grabbed two beers from the fridge, and handed one to Ray.

***

That night she woke to a full sitting position from a nightmare. Johnny told everyone at school what he had done and they all cornered her, calling out, "Freak, freak, freak. Are you a zombie Mara? What kinda freak are you Mara Taylor?" In distress, she panicked and transformed into the wolf in front of everyone and began attacking them all.

Bothered by her dream and more so by the fact it could happen if she didn't act soon, she got out of bed and ran out the backdoor. Taking on her wolf form, she headed into town towards Johnny's house. She wasn't sure what she was going to do when she got there but she knew she had to figure something out and soon.

Within minutes, she was looking at his house but she had no idea which window belonged to his room. She walked with her nose in the air trying to find a scent that would help her find him but she had no luck. Thinking about how his parents' room was probably at the front of the house, she went to the backyard. The curtains were dark and well lined but she knew the smaller, higher window had to be the bathroom so that only left two other windows. The one to the left probably belonged to a room attached to the kitchen so she went and looked at the window to her right. There was a small slit of an opening in the curtains and she stepped closer to the window to look into it. She could see a poster on the wall of the Dallas Cowboy's cheerleading squad scantily clothed and his clothes lay all over the floor, she recognized the jersey he'd worn earlier that day. She raised her paw up to the window and leaned into it a little. The glass gave way with a loud shatter and she took off running. Alarmed, Johnny jumped up and grabbed the bat he kept next to his bed. He walked toward the window, swinging the bat at it as he neared. His father walked in the room and upon seeing Johnny standing there with the bat hollered, "What the Hell?"

Johnny lowered the bat and his eyes, "I don't know, sir. I was asleep. Something woke me up and I..." Johnny put the bat down and sat on his bed, "I don't know." Johnny couldn't share his fears with his father because he'd have to admit what he'd done and he was never going to do that.

"You better get that cleaned up right now." His dad started pulling the door closed and then stuck his head back in the room, "You'll replace that window out of your pay. You hear me young man?"

"Yes Dad."

Chapter 13

Mara was careful to be quiet as she dressed and ate her breakfast. She wanted to avoid any conversation with her dad. It had been a trying night, her emotions were all over the place this morning and she didn't want anything to slip up in conversation. Johnny was hard on her mind and after the stunt she pulled, she was even more worried about him. It had been a mistake for her to go to his house. But, the nightmare was so real.

If she could just talk to Johnny, show him, then maybe she wouldn't have to fear being exposed. They could make some sort of a pact with each other. But, it took her nearly a week to accept this reality in her life. How could anyone else believe it? She couldn't find a way to tell one person much less her father and everyone else. Then there was her mother to consider. How could she explain about her mother? Would her dad be receptive to them being a family once he knew the truth? There was no way. No one could know. She couldn't possibly speak the words out loud to anyone.

Life would be a lot less complicated if Johnny just didn't exist, if no one knew anything about any of this. She was shocked at herself for the flash reaction of her mind. It was the next natural response in answer to the problem at hand, his existence. No, she couldn't do that. She didn't want to believe she even contemplated it.

She wanted to believe there was another way. There had to be. She couldn't take someone's life. But what if it was the only way?

She'd been driving around listlessly for fifteen minutes or so and she realized she was sitting at the mouth of Parkin's Road. She pulled her car onto the roadway and parked at the place where her life had taken its turn.

She turned off the car and sat while her mind stared into the headlights of Johnny's truck again.

He'd nearly done it, wiped her out of existence. Hitting her with his vehicle had been an accident but leaving her buried alive in a shallow grave had not. That night she had been his secret. A secret he was willing to bury and forget. Something he needed to keep hidden. She heaved forward and felt something tickle her cheek. She reached up to find tears on her face. Warmth, reminding her of the blood on her face that night. She began retching violently and opened the car door leaning over to vomit. When she was done, she cranked the car and headed for school.

She knew what she had to do and nausea hit her again. She realized the choice she was making meant she was going to be no better a person than he'd been that night.

All the conversations she'd shared with him in her mind had gone poorly. She hadn't been able to imagine a single one that wouldn't exasperate the situation. She really had no choice. She couldn't turn back the time and events that were in their past. She could only rid the world of the one person who could expose her.

***

Val smiled and waved good- bye to Eddie and Johnny. By the time she got to Mara, the dam of tears she had been fighting burst. She hurried into the car afraid Eddie would see her.

Once inside with the door closed, she blurted out, "Johnny, Johnny, Johnny! I'm so sick of him." "What is the deal with them?" Mara emphasized 'is'. She began to feel pangs of guilt for the cost Val was paying emotionally, but she quickly bit back, after all, if it weren't for Johnny neither of them would be in this position.

"I don't know. Johnny's dad gave Eddie a job, but they spend all their free time together now. I can't believe they leave football practice and work so late that he can't come over and spend thirty minutes with me." Her tears came harder and her nose was running. Mara didn't have any tissue and she knew Val needed some, so she pulled into McD's and ordered two medium cokes. She handed Val the napkins she'd requested at the window. Val gladly accepted them and began to wipe her tears and blow her nose. She continued, "Eddie and I have a date after the game tomorrow night. I guess I'll wait and see what happens. Maybe he's just too tired to come by after practice and work."

Mara understood Val trying to reason out Eddie's excuses. Val was so proud to be dating the quarterback and she genuinely cared for Eddie, but Mara had had enough of the situation herself. If it continued, Mara was never going to catch Johnny alone.

"Have you tried laying the law down to Eddie? Tell him you're tired of his not finding time for you and if he doesn't make your date tomorrow night you are through with him."

Val thought about it for a minute, "What if he doesn't? I don't want to break up with him, and if for some reason he can't make it he'll think I have."

"I don't think so Val. He's got a choice to make - it's you or Johnny. I'm sure Johnny and Julie are going out after the game. Julie will be free from her fund-raiser. What is Eddie gonna do? Hang out with Johnny and Julie? I don't think so. It's time for you to learn where you stand with him Val. Don't keep putting up with this."

Val could hear the frustration in her voice and was glad to have a friend who cared and understood so much. She didn't feel silly about her feelings anymore and she knew Mara was right. She was tired of wallowing in her self-pity over Eddie. "I'm gonna do it."

"I'm glad. So, you're gonna call and tell him tonight?"

"Yep."

Mara smiled at her, "Feel better?"

Val let out a small laugh, "Yea. Thanks Mara."

"No prob."

Mara breathed a sigh of relief and relaxed in her seat, *tomorrow night, I'll be watching him and I'll be waiting.*

Chapter 14

She watched the cheerleaders and the band as they smiled and cheered in their joy andcelebration. Team spirit was readily apparent in the colors of everyone's clothes and the banners splashed along the walls of the gymnasium. Balloons of orange and white cascaded through the air, as they fell from a box suspended above the basketball court. The mascot, a bulldog, ran through a poster bearing the picture of a Mustang as the band played, "Who Let the Dogs Out" and the cheerleaders whooped and slammed their pompoms at the air.

It was so surreal to her. She envied everyone around her for the lives they were living. The life she was supposed to have, not this half-life. They didn't live a life they had to keep to themselves, buried down deep inside. Oh sure some of them may be holding a secret but she just knew none of them had to keep one as deep as the one she held. Mostly she knew none of them would have to kill someone to keep it.

It was harder to be the girl hiding the wolf inside her than it was to be the wolf. The choice her mother made not to return home had been the easiest way to live but she just could not bear to think of leaving her dad alone. She had dreams, normal human events that would happen in her life, things like this, pep rallies, and boyfriends, dances, and graduation. No,

Johnny's actions robbed her of all her life should be but she was going to make sure he would keep his mouth shut. Once he was gone, no one else would ever know. She was going to have her life, the one she'd planned and her dad wasn't going to lose her like he had her mother. There would be no turning back on this decision.

The members of the football team took the court one by one, as their names blared from speakers over the gymnasium. Julie and the other cheerleaders bounced around and waved their pompoms, touching their hands and feet together as they did so. Val and Mara sat in the stands watching and applauding with the rest of the student body and staff.

"So did you give Eddie the ultimatum?" Mara asked as the band played the school's alma mater.

"Yep. He apologized. He said Johnny's family had gotten a couple of big jobs and they'd been busy, that he really hadn't been trying to ignore me."

"I'm sure that made you feel a little better but I hope you don't give in to him later if he calls and tries to put you off again."

"Nope. No way. I've come this far standing up for myself. There's no way I'm standing down now."

"Good. That's the attitude you need to have about it. You just keep that up."

They continued watching the players tossing the football around and the cheerleaders praising them. Val looked over at Mara, "Have I told you how much I enjoy our friendship."

"No you haven't." Mara said seriously, then smiled at her, "Of course you have. You are the girl who rarely leaves herself unspoken."

"I'm telling you again then. It's real nice havin' someone to hang with while they're busy with practices and games."

"I've enjoyed it too Val. I'm kinda worried what's gonna happen to us after football season is over."

"I'll work it out. You don't worry about that." Val held up her pinky, and Mara wrapped one of her pinkies around it, "BFF's" and they smiled together. "You gonna need a ride to the game tonight?" Mara asked.

"No, I'm gonna ride with Eddie. He says if I'm with him when the games over Johnny won't expect him to hang around."

"Good idea." Mara was as glad about that for Val's sake, as she was in knowing that she may finally catch Johnny alone.

***

That night Mara said good-bye to Val and left after the game like everyone else. She drove two blocks over and parked in the darkness of a wooded area leading up to the field house. With her black car hidden in the darkness, she began to let her emotions take over. All the anger she held for Johnny she could now let herself feel in a way she had had to repress before. There was no more debating about sparing his life, it was all too clear to her from her nightmare that he couldn't be trusted to keep what happened a secret forever. At the first muscle contraction, she got out of the car and took her clothes off, placing them in her seat. She slammed the door shut a little harder than she meant to and ran off through the woods stopping at the edge of the field.

Johnny pleaded, "Come on Eddie. Can't you take just thirty minutes of your time to help me put up all this equipment and we can get out of here together?"

"No man, I'm sorry. I was a no show the other night with Val because of you. Now she's waiting for me and I'm not going to make her sit and watch while we pick up this equipment. What's your problem anyway? You're worse than the girls, not wanting to be alone and all."

"Nothing. Never mind. You just go on and go. Don't worry about me. I'll make it to Julie's when I make it there. Just go on." Johnny kicked a helmet and walked away with his hands on his hips.

Eddie threw his hands up in the air, "Man I'm sorry, but I'm not making Val mad at me again this week!" He turned around and headed to his car. He could see Johnny bagging up the football gear as he left.

Mara watched as Johnny kicked a few more items and spit. She had wanted this all week and now that the moment was here, she wondered if she could do it. Just as she had never presumed she would be left to die at sixteen, she surely never considered taking the life of anything before, not the animals she had killed, especially not a person. She knew the only way she could do this was to let the wolf take over completely just as it had done when she was hungry. This was another act of desperation and he was nearly done picking everything up. She slipped out of her humanity and let go in a deep howl, as he stood up with the bag, Mara lunged onto him knocking him down onto his back. She placed her front paws on his chest and looked into his frightened eyes. The glow in her eyes brightened, as she smelled the fear emanating from him. The kind of fear she had the night their paths crossed for the first time. Fear created by the realization of one's mortality, a paralyzing desperation.

Johnny cried out and she stepped off him. Adrenaline forced his body to roll over, get up and head off in a dead run. But the wolf was faster. In one stride, its run turned into a leap and its jaws were around his head, biting down. She felt his head relax and roll forward as he went unconscious. She dropped him and nudged his torso to roll him over. Clamping her teeth into his neck, she did not let go until she tasted the rich blood pouring from his jugular vein.

She raised her head and looked at him one last time before running back through the woods to her car.

Nora heard the howl and ran to its direction. When she arrived at the field, Mara was gone but she found

Johnny's body in the field. She stood over him in shock. *Oh God Mara, what have you done?* She had been so proud of her for handling this curse so well. She was glad to see Mara take control of it. She never imagined Mara could take someone's life, but here it was. She knew she had to confront her about it.

***

Julie could not believe Johnny was standing her up. He'd been spending entirely too much time with Eddie. When he was with her, his mind was elsewhere and she may as well not even been present. She knew it wasn't something she'd done but when she tried to get him to talk about it, he'd just get mad and leave like he was angry. *If he doesn't show up soon,* she pouted, *I'll just go out without him. I don't have to put up with this, and if he doesn't want to talk about it with me I'm not going to let him continue to punish me with it.* She looked at her phone and saw it was 10:30; he was already forty-five minutes late. She punched in his number and listened to it ring several times before she decided to call Val.

"Hey is Johnny with Eddie?"

"No Julie, we're waiting on you guys up here at Pia's."

"Well, I don't know what's going on. He hasn't shown up and apparently he's ignoring my phone calls. Does Eddie know where he is?"

"Hold on," Val put the phone away from her face and Julie heard her relay their conversation to Eddie. He took the phone, "Julie, I left Johnny at the ball field. He had pick up duty. The last time I saw him he was bagging gear to carry into the field house. Course, he was angry at me because I wouldn't stay and help."

"Just because he was mad at you is no reason to stand me up. I mean what is his deal lately?"

"I don't know but he's been acting like he's afraid of something. He's been more needy and clingy than any girlfriend I've ever had." Eddie laughed and tugged at Val's hair, winking at her.

"Well, I think I'll call and see if he's home. I want to know what's going on. I am tired of his acting this way and he'll talk to me or else I'm done with him." Julie was nearly in tears.

She tried calling Johnny's phone again but still there was no answer. She was infuriated he wouldn't answer her calls.

She decided to check with his parents, maybe he was home ignoring her. At this point, she could care less if it angered him.

"Mr. Thomson, this is Julie. Is Johnny there?"

"No, he told me he had a date with you after the game."

"Yeah, well he hasn't shown up yet." Julie let out a big sigh, "Mr. Thomson, it's none of my business, but is everything okay with Johnny? He's been kinda distant lately and he won't talk to me about what's going on." She waited out the pause.

"Julie he's seemed fine to me. Something was going on with Eddie. Johnny asked me to give him a job for a while and I did. Those boys have been busy though, with football practice, studies, and work. I'll go to the field house and check on him if it'll make you feel better."

Julie thought about it for a minute and added with a note of pained smartness, "No. Thanks anyway but I'm sure he's alright where ever he's at."

"Okay. I am sorry he hasn't called you with a reason though. I'll have a talk with him about his manners when I see him.

"Thanks Mr. Thomson. You have a good night."

"You too, Julie."

As he hung up the phone, Mr. Thomson looked at the clock. It was 11:20. He contemplated checking on Johnny but he knew his son could be asleep in his truck in the school parking lot. It wouldn't be the first time he'd done it. He decided to wait until after his curfew.

***

Ray's phone rang at one o'clock Saturday morning. Startled out of his sleep, he reached over to his nightstand knocking the receiver to the floor with his flailing hand. He sat up and noticed the clock as he reached down to pick it up.

"Ray? Jack. Listen I need you up here at the high school. It's the Thomson boy, and it looks like some kind of an animal attack."

"Is he okay?" Ray rubbed his eyes trying to wake up.

"No, he's dead. His throat's been ripped out so bad his head was nearly torn from his body. And his head...I've never seen anything like it."

"Oh my God!" Ray whispered as he gripped the side of the bed. "There's not an animal in our region capable of doing that to a man."

"I know, that's why I need you to get on this. Ray, you just gotta see this. I...I don't know what we're looking at here..." Jack sounded shocked and at a loss for further words.

"Okay, I'll be there in half an hour."

"Alright, we'll hold 'til you get here."

Ray removed his clothes from the hook on the back of his door and put them on. On his way to the bathroom to wash his face, he looked into Mara's room. Her bed was empty. He didn't have time for this. Why didn't she come home when she was supposed to and how was he going to handle this. He knew it was too soon to give her so much freedom. Right now there was a dead boy on their school property, some kind of wild animal on the loose and that was priority. He'd deal with her later.

Chapter 15

Jack, Marks, and Mr. Thomson were standing on the sideline as the medical examiner stood waiting over Johnny. "Jack." Ray hollered as he stepped out of the truck.

They met each other on the way out to the field. "Ray I don't know what to tell Bill. He got a call from Johnny's girlfriend last night because she thought Johnny was standing her up for date. After they got off the phone, he decided to wait until Johnny was late for his curfew to look for him. Ray, he's really kicking his self in the ass right now. He thinks if he'd come earlier Johnny would be okay."

"What did the medical examiner say?"

"He says Johnny's been like this for at least two hours, give or take a half an hour. It's hard to be more definite than that." Jack watched as Ray examined Johnny's wounds. Ray shook his head, "Doesn't help how Bill's feeling much, huh?"

"No." Jack put his hands on his hips, "Have you ever seen anything like it?"

Ray stood up and wiped his forehead, "No. This doesn't make any sense." He reached over and down, lifting some hairs gathered on Johnny's jersey.

"These hairs are canine. Let me see your flashlight."

Ray reached out, took Jack's flashlight and turned it on to get a better look at the hairs, "They are black and grey or silver."

He looked around at the ground walking from Jack towards the woods. When he spotted the first tracks, the hairs on his neck, back and head stood as if he had just walked through an electrical field. The tracks were deeper than any he had ever seen and the distance between them told him the animal was one of great height and the paws themselves were larger than his hands. He knew of no canine animal that would leave such tracks, not even a wolf. But, that's what he was seeing and in his hand, he knew he held the fur of a wolf.

He turned around to look at Jack and the medical examiner, glad for the dark distance between them, glad they could not see the expression in his face, the look in his eyes. As he approached them, he gathered himself.

"It's definitely an animal attack and it's definitely not anything common to our region."

"Well, that was my thinking. So I figured I needed you to see this and find out what we got loose out here."

Ray wondered if he was going to be any help. He didn't even know for sure if he could believe such an animal existed. "I'll check the local exotics registry when the county offices open. I'll give you a call and let you know if I find anything there."

Jack told the medical examiner to remove Johnny's body and he and Ray headed back to Marks and Bill Thomson. "Bill, this is Ray Taylor. Ray, this is Johnny's father, Bill Thomson." The two men shook hands and Johnny's father grabbed Ray by his arm, "Please, please find out what did this to my boy."

"I will do my best Mr. Thomson." Ray felt helpless and his heart went out to Bill. He remembered it was around a week ago, when he believed himself to be the father who'd lost a child to murder or death.

Mara, he had to get home and see if she'd gotten back. "Jack, I gotta go," he took off running to his truck, "I'll call ya in a while."
Ray's behavior and swift departure startled Jack, "Ray is everything alright?"
"Yeah, yeah gotta go. I'll call ya."

***

Ray was relieved to see Mara's car in the driveway when he arrived home. He checked her room before going to the kitchen to put on a pot of coffee. She was fast asleep. Relieved he walked over to her bed and watched her as she slept. He felt so lucky to have her home safe. He noticed the scar on the side of her face and said a prayer of thanks, grateful that was the worst of what happened to her. He decided to let her sleep. He would deal with her when she got out of bed. He pulled her door slightly closed before going downstairs.
Right now, he was going to drink his coffee, get good and awake and go track a killing beast. More drama was the last thing he needed. He could hardly get the picture out of his mind of the dead boy's injuries. Chills still set in when he imagined the animal that could have done it. After three cups of coffee, he rounded up his trap and a flashlight and headed back to the football field to start his tracking.
For two hours, he followed tracks through the woods almost all of them around the creek bed. When he realized he was only about a half mile from his house, it caused him some uneasiness. He lifted the flax canvas backpack and pulled it off his shoulder. After unzipping it, he removed the pieces of pine branches, which he used for scent concealment. Next, he set out the trap and tools he needed. He used a mallet to drive the chain's stake in the ground. He placed the trap in the print; he slid his leather setters over each side of the trap and pulled them apart. He was careful not to disturb the trip pad as he covered the trap with dead leaves.

***

She'd driven home last night with all of her windows
down. She wanted the wind to blow through and
around her, to blast away what she'd done. She
simply wanted to forget it. She reasoned with herself
that Johnny would have done the same as she'd done.
Although her's was an intentional act and his behavior
had been preceded by an accident, but wasn't their
motive the same?

Even as she lay in bed on this new day, rationalization
was failing her. She wondered how long guilt would
be her companion.

She listened as her father's truck left the gravel
driveway and hummed on the pavement toward
town. She knew they had probably discovered
Johnny's body by now, and that her father had been
called in for assistance. By the end of the day, half the
men in town would probably be looking for the animal
that killed Johnny.

Right now her biggest fear was facing the
consequences and punishment her dad would lay on
her for not being home on time last night. She
dressed hastily, grabbed her keys. She wanted to go
and find out if anyone knew about Johnny yet.

She had her answer before she pulled in the
driveway. Val was sitting on the porch with her head
in her hands. Mara quickly got out of her car and
offered her arms out in a hug to comfort her friend.

"I'm so glad you're here," Val said through her sobs,
"Eddie is at Julie's. He said she's just too devastated
to see me. Can you believe it? I am her best friend,
Mara. We've been best friends for three years and
Eddie is gonna tell me I can't be there because it's all
just too much for her right now."

"But he's there?" Mara asked incredulously. She
hated that things were turning out for Val like this but
she had to do what she'd done.

"Yeah. Maybe he really has been after Julie all along and I've just been the biggest idiot ever to believe in him."

Mara held Val as she cried. She felt pangs of guilt and remorse for using her the way she did. The knowledge that her actions caused Val this pain burdened her more. She wanted to fix it but how could she turn back time. "You know, you could be wrong. Just give it a little time and see what happens. They were the two closest to Johnny. Maybe that's all it is."

"I guess so. I mean that could be it."

Mara pushed Val back and smiled at her, "You wanna go riding around or shopping or something? Get your mind off this?"

"Yesssss. Just let me get myself fixed up. I'm sure the look of self-pity hasn't become the latest trend."

Mara's phone rang. She looked to see who was calling her and dreaded answering when she read 'daddy' on the display.

"Hey Dad"

"Mara where are you?" he was pretty upset she wasn't home on time last night but even more frustrated when he got home this morning and she was gone. Mara could hear the underlying anger in his voice and she lowered her head and lied to him again. "I'm at Val's. I'm sorry, she called me this morning and was upset. Daddy, Johnny was killed last night."

"I know honey," his tone lightened into a sad one, "I got called on the case this morning. You weren't here when I got up. Where were you Mara?"

"I'm sorry. We were just hanging out after the game and time got away from me. I didn't mean to be out so late. I'll try to be more careful, but Dad, Val really needs me right now."

"I understand. Just call me and let me know what's going on with you when you're out, so I don't have to worry so much."

"I will Daddy. I promise." A few minutes passed and Mara still wasn't sure exactly where she stood, "I love you Daddy."

"I love you too Mara. You come home before too late okay."

"I will. We're just gonna go to the theater and probably hang at the mall for a while. Try to get Val's mind off Eddie being at Julie's. They won't let Val be there and it's really tearing her up inside."

"Okay baby, you girls be careful."

"We will."

She pushed the "end button". She had lied. Since she had come home it seemed she had to tell lie after lie. She just wanted all of this to be over.

She hoped no one ever found her out, but running to take care of Val before hearing the news of Johnny's death from her dad had not been the smartest move. If anyone learned she'd never been told, it would be suspect. She knew she would have to put a lot more planning into her actions in the future.

Chapter 16

Mara no longer needed to spend her time stalking Johnny. Although life was full trying to comfort Val, she now had the nights to let the wolf take her over and begin looking for her mother.

She just wanted to see her, to be hugged by her and to hug her. She wanted to tell her she loved her, even after all this time. That she missed her so desperately. And, she wanted answers. How could this be, the thing she had been made?

She returned to the creek where she'd lost her mother's scent the last time she tried to track her. She crossed the creek bed to see if she could pick it up on the other side. Yes, it was there and it was heavy. She became excited, but she followed it carefully so she would not lose it again. She heard movement and looked in the direction of the sound. There sat her mother behind a blind she'd made of branches.

"Mara," she pointed to something across from her, "there is your blind, and you have to change. I really need to talk to you."

Mara paced giddily almost unable to contain her joy. "Come on girl, I need you to settle down. We have to talk," Nora spoke to her just the same as she had all those years ago. It was that, 'I love you, but you better do what I say' tone.

Mara walked behind the blind and lay down on her side. She began to breathe deeply and envision her meadow with the butterflies. She sat up on her legs and looked over the blind at her mother. "God Momma, I want to hug you so bad right now. Why didn't you come back to the cabin? I mean after I learned the truth about you. About us. I don't understand why you stayed away. I even looked for you but you were gone again."

"I know Mara."

"Please come home. I want you to come home and so does Dad. I can teach you Momma. I can teach you how to control the wolf. You can come home, Momma." Mara rattled as if time was running out on her. She never intended to put pressure on her mother to return home. She had reconciled with herself about the decision her mother made to stay away. Now here she was, confronting her mother about the possibility of having their family back together, trying to bargain with her to get her to come home.

"Sweetie, you have to know how strange it would be for me to come home. Come on baby, it has nearly been ten years. How would I explain where I have been? You've got to start thinking things through."

"Momma I know, but we want you home so bad. We miss you. I can't think about anything else right now except us being a family again. Your secret is safe Momma, I can help you," Mara cried.

"Mara, I can't, but I have been watching you. I guess you know that by now." Nora paused and remembered the years passed, "That I was there the night you were hit by the boy in the truck was no coincidence. What you may not know is that I was there the night you ended that boy's life. I was in disbelief you were capable of such an act, but there I was, standing over his dead body."

Mara interrupted, "Momma I had to, he knew about me, that I shouldn't be alive. I had to make sure he would never tell anyone. So you see Momma nobody has to know."

"No honey, you could have let him live in fear of you and the fear of people finding out what he'd done to you. Surely, that would have been enough to keep him quiet. Instead, you have put us in jeopardy. For years, there have been many of us living in small packs. My pack does not know of your existence and I hope to keep it that way. There is a code. We will do no harm to anyone, nor turn them. If we break that code, the penalty is death. Now there is an investigation into the boy's death. The type of wounds he died from was evident of an unusually large wild animal. I don't know what's going to come from that, but I am afraid for both of us now." Nora's face filled with a look of deep concern and Mara asked, "Mother, exactly what are we?"

"A few hundred years ago there was a shifter named Tala. One night while Tala was hunting, a werewolf attacked her and she lost her ability to shift into other creatures. No matter how hard she tried, a wolf was the only shift she was able to make. It was purely by accident that she learned a wound inflicted by her would create another like her.

Her movement startled a hunter, and as he aimed his rifle at her, she leapt and struck him down. A few days later, he showed up at her reservation looking for answers as to what she had done to him. He told her how quickly his wound had healed and of experiencing the transition of man to wolf, as she listened with fascination. Tala was happy to hear his story and saw it as an opportunity to strengthen the people of her tribe.

At first, she converted only her best hunters. Their stock of food and hides grew rapidly and that was good or so it seemed, until the Great Rite, when the elder men of the tribe took the boys approaching manhood on their Spirit journey. The men departed the village never to return. On the night of the fourth day, Tala shifted and ran to the site of their camp.

When she arrived she found the innocent of boys of her tribe slaughtered alongside their fathers and grandfathers. Bodies torn so badly at the limbs that she could not tell what belonged to whom, only that the way the men were ravaged was done by beasts. Beasts that she knew in that moment she had created. The guilt was so overwhelming she could not bear to face her tribe. The hunters she had passed the weir part of herself to were gone.

We are her descendants, a blend of shifter and werewolf. We are shifter in that we become a four-legged wolf, not one capable of standing and walking on its back legs, but we are larger and much more powerful than a normal wolf. We gained some werewolf gifts, you might say, but we also lost the choice to shift into anything other than a wolf. We are not controlled by the moon, most of the time we can control our wolf side but we are werewolf in our ability to pass the trait on to a victim wounded by us."

"Why didn't you come home when you learned you could control it?"

"I saw what happened with your Uncle Ernie and Aunt Katie. Mara, I was afraid of the same thing happening to us. The night I scratched you and made you a wolf was a decision made in haste and out of grief. I hoped the journal could prepare you for your new life but I shouldn't have been so hasty."

"What are you saying Momma? You should've let me die? Is that what you're saying?" Mara hollered in pain and disbelief.

"I don't know. I don't know... does it matter now? I did it. We are here and I'm not sure that meeting you has helped, but you are in danger Mara, and I'm so afraid for you."

Mara was so hurt, "You don't worry for me Momma. I've been fine since you left me and I'll be fine now. If I never see you again it'll be fine with me." She arose and ran off through the trees behind her. The change happened so fast she didn't even notice it this time.

When Mara jumped the creek-bed, her back right paw
triggered the trap's pad and a loud yelp escaped from
her throat. The excruciating pain radiated from just
above her paw and pushed itself up through the rest
of her body. She began to hack and gag as acid rose to
her throat from her stomach and a sour taste filled
her cheeks. She lay down and tried to fight the pain.
Mara knew she would have to shift back into human
form to release her foot but the physical and
emotional trauma she was in presented newer and
harder challenges for her. She began to howl in her
angst. On top of the fact that her mother had no plans
to come home, she faced the reality that her father
was hunting her.

The howling was faint, but it was audible to Ray as he
lay in a half sleep. He rose from his bed, grabbed his
shotgun and flash light, and headed across the yard
toward the woods. He was sure his trap had worked
and he was going to get Johnny's killer before it killed
again.

Chapter 17

Making the change to release herself was hopeless in this moment. The pain was too extreme, the anguish toward her mother was overwhelming her ability to think, but she knew she had to get free. She raised herself up and pulled at the chain, luckily it was not anchored strongly enough to match her power. She bolted up and ran on her three good legs carrying the injured one above the ground, dragging the trap's chain and anchor.

Not only had Ray heard her howl but Nora had also. She ran until she picked up the scent of her daughter and followed it to find Mara lying on the ground, licking at her bloody paw. She approached carefully and tried to help, but Mara glared at her and gave a low guttural growl. Nora backed up a step and sat with a whimper. Mara snarled and growled again, this time more fiercely. Nora stood and turned with her head down. Once she disappeared through some brush, Mara began to try focusing.

She was a young girl at the meadow and her foot was throbbing from a bumblebee sting. She placed her foot in the meadow's pond so the water could soothe her sting. It felt so cool and so nice. She began to feel her body relaxing and she was conscious of the changing. She took a deep breath and opened her eyes. She felt the pain again in her leg. She sat up and reached the trap with her hands, pulled the trap's jaws open and carefully lifted her foot out of it. She slowly let the trap snap shut. Now she had to get home as quickly as possible, undetected.

***

Ray shined his light towards the creek and looked to the group of trees where he had set the trap. Spotting a particular knotted pine, he approached slowly even though he saw no creature or movement. He aimed the light on the ground. The trap was gone, but there was a drag mark and some blood spots leading away from the area. He wiped his forehead with his hands, adjusted the shoulder strap on his shotgun, and set out to follow the trail.

Nora followed Mara's scent back towards the house. She travelled cautiously, aware there may be more snares lying in wait. There was a sound. A small branch breaking and a rustle in the time measure not of any deer or animal she'd heard. She raised her nose and drew in a good breath. It was a man. And not just any man. It was Ray and he was close.

Nora knew she needed to act quickly. She had to buy Mara time to free herself and get home. She ran noisily, circling through trees, trying to draw him in, trying to draw him away from Mara. She paused and listened. It worked. She could hear his footsteps approaching and she carried her circle further out to draw him even more. She led him deeper into the woods, stopped and hid, watching as he searched until she felt Mara had had time to escape the trap and make it home. She had watched Mara at the cabin after the change, learning to control the wolf inside of her and she knew Mara could handle herself. When Nora felt it had been long enough, she stepped from behind the tree and into a clearing. Ray cowered in horror as the wolf's body came slowly into his view and his heart stopped when it lifted its head and peered at him. Its eyes glowed even more in the glare of his flashlight. He tried to make his legs move but they were part of the ground, simply immobile. He felt the weight of his shotgun on his shoulder but he was too afraid to move. The wolf turned away from him and disappeared into the darkness.

He dropped to the ground. The flashlight shook in his hand as he held it up to look into the eerie darkness of the woods. He listened but all he could hear was the beating of his own heart. Once the muscles in his body relaxed, he stood and began his walk back home, looking behind him a few times. Everything seemed calm until one of his feet cracked a branch. He took off running. Praying the wolf wasn't returning for him.

He ran nearly all the way to the house until he got in sight of its light, then he heard the screen door on the back porch shut. He hoped it was Mara, awake and looking for him, but if it wasn't, he needed to be there. Once inside he found no lights on and no sounds. He carefully walked through the kitchen to the living room before making his way upstairs to look in on her. She was in her bed with her back turned to him. He watched as her covers moved up and down with the rhythm of her breathing. She was fine and he was relieved. He had not noticed anything out of the ordinary, but he checked the house once more.

***

Mara waited for him to go to bed before she looked at her ankle. The trap's jaws had nearly reached the bone. She remembered the injuries she suffered from the impact of Johnny's truck and how quickly she had healed once she received what her mother had given her. What her mother had given her, a curse or a gift? She didn't know. She lay back and pondered that question until sleep came to her.

She dreamed of her meadow, of her mother and father being there with her and they were all three wolves.

Running and playing in the field. They hunted together, one small, happy pack.

She wondered upon waking if it was wrong to wish her dream was true. Was it so wrong to pass this on to another just to be a family again? How would her father handle the gift, the truth?

She was drawn back to reality by her father's announcement from the kitchen, "Mara, breakfast is ready."

She sat up in bed and looked at her ankle. It was bruised and tender but it was not bleeding, and the skin was not broken as it had been the night before. She stood up on it, preparing herself for the pain she expected to feel, but it wasn't that bad, so she tried walking across her room. There was just a slight need to be gentle on it. She would have a little limp, nothing too hard to explain, and certainly nothing to alert her dad to make him suspect she had stepped into his trap.

When she entered the kitchen, he noticed her care in her walking and the favoring of her left leg. "What happened to your foot?"

"I was walking up onto the porch last night and I guess I didn't get my foot on the last step very good."

"Good going grace," he knelt down before her and began to examine the bruises and rotate the ankle feeling the bones. She giggled when it hurt a little, "That's what I said as I sat on my butt looking up at the porch." She smiled at her dad.

"You better wrap that up in the ace bandage from the medicine cabinet. It's sprained pretty good. If it's not better in a few days we should probably let Doc have a look at it."

She finished the last bite of her toast, "I'll wrap it, but I'm sure Doc won't have to check it out."

Chapter 18

Nora knew she had put Mara in even more danger by exposing herself to Ray. The wounds inflicted on Johnny which ultimately caused his death were already enough to endanger her pack. She could no longer keep what she'd done a secret. She was going to have to admit it to the Elders.

It had been ten years since they last faced such an atrocity committed by a pack member, the attack of Nora. An action taken by Sid, a member who was rogue, he disagreed with the pack's views and laws. He took it upon himself to leave and try to form his own pack. His plans may have succeeded had it not been for Evan finding Nora.

Through her, they learned of Sid's attempt with Ernie and had it not been for Nora's anger over her family, Sid may have accomplished his goal. They acted swiftly to go to the cabin area, an area Sid planned to use as his pack base. According to the pack laws, he was an abomination. The members of the pack believed themselves to be unnatural, cursed. A curse that was a mortal sin to pass to another. A sin that literally led to Sid's beheading.

Upon arriving at pack territory, she took on her human form and called out, "Counsel."

Seven grey wolves appeared around her and rose as men and women. They sat surrounding her and she took her place on the ground at center. The oldest of the counsel spoke first, "Why have you called us here?"

"I have made a terrible mistake. A mistake that puts my daughter in danger and possibly even our existence."

"What is this mistake?"

"I found my daughter at death's door. I passed on the shift to save her."

A collective sigh permeated the air, and she felt the heaviness of their disappointment and her shame.

"You know it is a sin against nature to interfere with fate. A power greater than ourselves predetermines our lives and there are consequences to usurping the One."

"Yes, I know," she began to weep, "I acted in haste. My daughter lay in front of me bleeding, barely hanging to life. It was more than I could bear. I was watching her slip away before my eyes and I couldn't let her go again." She shuddered and wiped her eyes, "I just got her back."

A woman interjected, "How do you mean, you just got her back?"

"Her father sent her away after my disappearance."

The head of the counsel cleared his throat, "How do you know all this? How many of our laws have you broken?"

Afraid to answer, she lowered her head as far as she could. Whispers roared in her ears. "I'm sorry. I'm so sorry." She said loud enough to try and silence the noise, "I have not stayed away from my home. I have traveled there several times out of concern for my husband. It is one thing for my mind to know to stay away, but the will of my heart became so strong at times that I ached to see him. I have only seen my daughter there a handful of times and only on the weekends. But a few weeks ago, she returned to our home and her things were in the back of Rays' truck. I hung around and waited to see more of them together. I was watching the night she left the house for a walk and a boy driving a pick-up truck hit her. I watched him load her into the bed of his truck and I followed him as he drove her into the woods. Once there he placed her in a shallow grave and left her to die." Tears streaming from her eyes, she raised her head and pleaded, "Please help? I need your help."

The pack leader's eyes pierced the darkness, "Why didn't you bring her to us? You know the laws."

"Yes I know the laws. There are two, which apply here. One, which says we may not try to live amongst humans and the one that says that I have committed a crime punishable by death. Neither entered my mind as I watched my daughter's life slipping away. Afterwards I carried her to the cabin where my life became what it is now. I watched as she taught herself how to control it and I left her only to check on Ray. I saw him suffering through her disappear-ance. The idea of him losing her for good and never knowing why was more than I could stand. I let her go. I let her go home and believed she could be safe. In my grief I acted in haste, and in my sorrow, I acted without forethought of the actions she'd have to take to protect us to keep the truth hidden."

"And what action do you speak of?"

"She took the life of the boy who left her for dead."
A loud grumble erupted. The pack leader rose to
silence the pack. He looked down at Nora, "You must
leave us now and await our request for your return.
We will now decide what must be done."
"Please?" Nora pleaded again, fearing that she and
Mara both faced the penalty of death for their actions,
but the pack leader raised his voice, "You have acted
on your own, and against this counsel. Now you will
leave us and let us find resolution."
Nora leaned forward and shifted back into wolf form;
she lowered her head and put her tail between her legs
stopping at the wood's edge to give one last pleading
whimper before disappearing into the trees.
The pack leader again sat down and looked at the
other six elders before finding the words to pro-ceed.
 "This matter calls for serious contemplation but in
need of a quick resolution. I'm sure I am not alone in
conflicting emotions. I also know that we should try
to leave our emotions out of this. After all, it is
emotion which has brought us to the necessity of this
moment."
The eldest woman sat at his right hand, she reached
over and placed her left hand on his knee, "But given
the same turn of events, who of us could say we would
not have done the same?"
Three elders' hands raised, all men. One of them
spoke, "To act in haste is a sign of weakness, a loss of
control. We cannot afford to be weak. We must stay
in control of our emotions. Although we possess the
power to bring a human out of the grip of death, we
are not as wise as the One. He is the Almighty and
knows all things past, present and future. He is the
only one who is truly worthy to possess power and let
others' fates be determined. He is able to speak to

others subconscious minds, an ability we do not possess. We have no control over anyone other than ourselves; therefore, it is true that we should leave another's fate to the One. She should have said her good-bye and let fate be done."

"You speak the truth of our beliefs but you have never had the blessed womb or given life to that blessing. It makes the matter much different for a mother."

The leader nodded in agreement with the eldest woman. She continued, "I can't condemn Nora to death for her actions, but I do feel it is necessary to give her the time to correct her actions. She must bring Mara to the pack."

"Yes, I think that would do." The eldest woman sighed.

"We will vote on this decision now." The pack leader began the voting by raising his hand, and five others followed by raising theirs. The vote passed, the leader called out for Nora. She returned to the circle, shifting to human form as she approached, she sat and faced the leader.

"You are going to be spared and given the chance to correct your hasty actions. We have decided you will bring Mara to the pack. If you cannot do this in the next few months or another becomes hurt or killed, we will have to take action. The member we place into her world will act in whatever will be necessary to keep others protected. Do you understand what I mean?"

"Yes, Elder." She spoke softly and hoped the 'necessary' would not happen.

"The quicker you bring Mara to the pack the better for her. Time is not a friend in an emotional world."

"I understand."

The elders leaned forward, becoming wolves, and left
Nora alone with her thoughts.

She knew there was no way to protect Ray from the
loss of Mara. However, if Mara stayed and he
continued to hunt her, something far worse would
happen. He would be standing over Mara's dead body
with the realization that he took her life.

Nora wasn't sure how she was going to get Mara to
come with her, but she knew it was the only way to
save her. She felt she needed to take some kind of
action to protect Mara from the pack while she tried
to re-open their communication.

She remembered the Owen's, a family she'd met when
two boys riding their four wheelers through the woods
found her unconscious moments after she suffered a
severe gunshot wound from a hunter. They put her on
the back of one of their ATV's and carried her to their
parents. Becca Owens, the mother took care of her
through the night.

Nora was surprised to wake up and find herself
clothed and in a bed. Becca sat in a chair next to the
bed reading. Nora tried to tell Becca that they had
placed themselves in danger by bringing her home.
She told her the story of Ernie and Katie and about
her attack but Becca just shushed her and wiped her
forehead with a cool rag. She decided Becca probably
believed she was crazy just as she herself wondered
about Katie's sanity when she talked about Ernie.

The next morning, Nora was well and ready to go,
afraid to stay another moment. The door opened and
pushed her hand back as she reached for the handle,
Becca entered the room carrying a plate of breakfast.
"I thought you'd be hungry this morning. Do you
want to eat in here or come on in the kitchen?"

Nora was stunned that Becca was not shocked to find her out of bed and doing well, "I guess I'll eat in here, if that's really okay?"

"Sure it is. Here you just sit right back down and eat. I'm going to clean the kitchen. If you'd like some more, it's in there."

"Thanks," Nora said, as she took the food from Becca and placed it in her lap.

Becca paused at the door and turned her head back toward Nora, "and that stuff you told me about last night?"

Nora nodded her head, "I know crazy, huh?"

Becca smiled gently, "Well when you're done with breakfast, I'd like to sit and talk with you about it."

Nora didn't understand why Becca would want to hear a story again that seemed crazy enough the first time. She wondered why Becca had not asked her what she was doing so deep in the woods, and naked to boot. Suddenly, she realized she was the only one who seemed curious about anything right now, and that was amusing. They had not asked her name nor had they recognized her. Of course, she had been missing for over eight years now and it is possible they had not lived in the area back then. She hurried the rest of her meal and left the room to find the kitchen. Becca was at the table with her husband. "Good morning."

He stood and took the empty plate from her and placed it into the sink as he introduced himself. "I'm John."

He held his hand out and Nora shook it, "Nora."

"Becca said it was a pretty frantic night for ya."

"Yes, I suppose it was. I'm sure I made it difficult for her when all I could do was insist I needed to leave."

"No. It wasn't a problem. Not at all." Becca said, a comforting smile on her face, "Why don't you sit down and tell John the story you tried to tell me last night. About what happened at your sister's cabin?"

Nervous about repeating something so unbelievable, and to top it off tell it to a man, was very scary to her but she felt obligated. She began with Katie's story about Ernie, and then told what happened to them, and she ended with her attack.

When she was done, John and Becca looked away from her and to each other. She panicked, "I know it's unbelievable but I promise you I don't need to be institutionalized."

They stood from the table and held hands, "Come outside with us."

She followed them out to the front porch. John let go of Becca's hand and put his hands on Nora's shoulders facing her. "You sit right here on this porch and watch. Don't panic though, just watch and be patient. Okay?"

She wasn't sure what they were going to do, but she agreed by nodding her head and sitting on the edge of the porch. John and Becca turned and walked away from her and almost in the blink of an eye, they were a cat and a dog. The two animals turned back to face her and walked to the porch. They jumped up and sat one on each side of her. As she looked away from the dog back to the cat she saw Becca sitting next to her and she turned back to look at the dog to see John again.

"Shifters?" she asked in a whisper. They laughed, "Yes," Becca answered, "so, we don't think you're crazy at all."

"We can be any animal we like. Any time. Comes in pretty handy, too." John laughed again. "Like when a stranger comes over. We just shift into a pack of dogs and bark angrily at the door. Works every time."

"How?" Nora asked, "I mean, what...?"

"Don't really know. Just been in our family genes for generations so far back nobody really remembers anything being any different." John answered.

John put two fingers in his mouth and whistled loudly. Two German Shepherds came running from behind the trailer, one tumbling over the other playfully, and then they rose up and two boys stood before her.

"Tyler and Skylar." Becca introduced them, "They found you yesterday and brought you here."

The boys smiled and bowed playfully, "Glad to see you better." Tyler told her.

"Thank you." Nora smiled, a little embarrassed that they had been the ones to find her in such a vulnerable state and with no clothes.

They were good-looking kids, Tyler with his dark hair and green eyes and Skylar with blonde hair, brown eyes and a dimple in his chin that disappeared when he smiled.

Both were around the same age as Mara. She wrapped her arms around herself, how she missed her daughter.

Becca saw the sadness in her eyes, "You fellas run on now and let us women folk visit." She stood up and reached down for Nora's hand, Nora put her hand in Becca's and pulled herself to stand. John and his boys shifted back into dogs and began frolicking with each other as the women went back in the trailer.

Mara needed someone on her side, people who would understand her and protect her from her dad and anyone else that may harm her. The Owens family could take care of her. Nora was sure of that.

Chapter 19

Becca answered the door to find Nora tugging at the dress she wore.

"Sorry," Nora blushed at being found in her discomfort, "not used to clothes. They're a little confining, huh?"

Becca laughed at her, "Yes, they are." She opened the door wider and invited Nora inside. They sat at the kitchen table. Nora put her hands in her lap and bowed her head as she began to pour out the reason for her visit, "I have a daughter."

"Yes, I know. I saw her on the news. I saw your story on there also. Are you sure it's safe for you to be here? I mean like this." Becca reached over and lifted Nora's face to look into her eyes. She saw the desperation and sorrow that lay behind them. Nora began to cry. Becca moved her hand from Nora's chin, "I'm so sorry. That must have seemed so cold of me."

"No. It's okay. I understand. I'm usually hanging around the property where Mara and Ray live, so that I can watch my family. I mean I can't be with them and that is hard enough but at least I can make sure they are okay. Every weekend I was there watching my daughter grow up. That's what I was doing when T.O. and Skylar found me here. It was during one of Mara's weekend visits with her father. Anyway, I was there the first night she went missing. I saw what happened to her. After that I became responsible for the rest of the time she was missing."

Becca interrupted, "How can that be?"

"I turned her. I gave her the wolf curse and now she may end up dead because of it. So you see I cannot be afraid for myself right now, of being discovered. I have to protect my daughter any way I can."

Becca sat in astonishment. "How?" She stammered, "I mean why? Why would you do that Nora? You call it a curse and you did it to your own daughter." She rose from the table and got them each a glass of water before sitting back down. "So was it an accident or something you had to do to save her life?"

"Both I guess." Nora took a drink and swallowed hard before continuing, "I can't tell you what happened, Becca. I know I should be able to tell you but I just can't."

"It's okay," Becca averted her eyes from Nora as she spoke her suspicion, "We watch the news and the boys go to the same school as the other kids around here. I've heard the stories about the boy they found on the school field. Was it Mara?"

"Yes." Nora sighed, "But she had to. He hit her and he believed she'd died. How could she explain her miraculous return if he said anything to anyone? If only I had let things happen the way they should have that night. If only I had not been so desperate to save her and I told her so last time I spoke to her. That was a mistake because now she is angry with me. Angry that I told her that I should have let her die. I don't think she is going to talk to me again. I need to get her to come to the pack with me but how can I if she will not talk to me? I went to them for help but they are insistent that I bring her in and if I do not...I don't know. It's just bad and I'm very afraid for her."

Becca listened in silence and when Nora was done, she reached across the table, took the hands of her crying friend into her own, and asked, "So, she was in an accident or something and you had to do it to save her life?"

"Yes, but I can't give you any more information about what happened to her that night. I hope that won't be a problem between us."

"I'm not gonna tell you that I don't want to know, but if you don't want to talk about it right now that's fine, I guess. It's your daughter and I understand you want to protect her, but how can we help?"

Nora sighed in relief, "Can you watch and protect her?"

"Yes Nora. We can do that. I'm sure John would be happy to help. The boys already go to school with her and can help us. She'll be fine. You quit worrying, okay. We won't let anyone harm your girl."

Nora wiped her nose on the back of her hand, "Thank you Becca."

Chapter 20

The weeks following Johnny's death, Mara stayed close to Val as much as possible while they watched the relationship between Eddie and Julie grow. Led partly by guilt but mostly by their friendship she tried to keep her busy and remind her that Eddie was no good and there would be other boyfriends. The first week Val was nearly inconsolable. Watching Eddie and Julie be the center of everyone's attention at the memorials and games didn't help matters.

Mara did not go to look for her mother again. That was her pain and she felt it was only fair she was suffering too. Her mother's words cut deeply. To know that not only was she never planning to come home, but also because she felt she should have just let Mara die. Mara cried several nights, wondering how her mother could be so cold. The same woman who gave birth to her, nursed her and raised her for six years. The same woman who kissed her goodnight and sang her to sleep. How could that woman be so cold after getting her daughter back, after finding hope they could be a family again? Mara knew in her heart the relationship between them was over, just as

Val and Eddie's was over, now she just needed to reconcile in her mind.

Things were changing just as they always do after a tragedy and there was no turning back, you just had to adapt. At least she and Val still had their friendship, as long as Val never learned the truth about Johnny's death.

**

All the orange and white ribbons bearing Johnny's number printed on small footballs began to disappear as the town tried to move on from the tragedy.

There was still much talk in the town and the local paper as to what happened that night, whether or not there was still need to fear an animal in the area or if it had possibly moved on to another town or county. People were clearly aggravated there were no answers to their questions. Some of the town's hunters were concerned for their safety and some were looking forward to spotting and killing the beast to be the town hero.

At school, the students just wanted to get back to life as usual. Mara's Biology class held another change they would face. A new teacher was writing on the chalkboard, a striking red head whose hair dropped the full length of her back, accenting her small waistline.

Once everyone was in their seats and the bell rang, she turned and gazed over her class with her deep teal eyes. "Hello class, my name is Ms. Karen. Ms. Clark is taking some time off and I am looking forward to teaching you." Her voice was as beautiful as her face and her accent was one of Irish or Scottish, Mara could rarely distinguish the two but she loved listening to both. Ms. Karen picked up her attendance book and began to call out names marking the book as each student replied.

Over the next week, pretty much everyone in Ms. Karen's classes decided she was indeed as cool as she was beautiful. She soon became the new topic with everyone. If you were in her class, you talked about how much fun she was and if you weren't in her class, you talked about how you were going to take one of her classes next semester.

Mara and Val always looked forward to her class because the special projects she assigned them, made learning more interesting than their other classes. Today they were turning in the insects they hunted and captured along with the research they'd written about their bugs. They had fun trying to find the most unusual bugs, Mara captured a stick bug and Val was lucky enough to capture a luna moth.

They finished their presentations just as the bell rang. The students stood to leave and Ms. Karen called Mara and Val to her desk, "I was very impressed with your choice of insects and your projects were unique from those of the other students. I need two assistants after school today to set up for tomorrow's class. I'd like for the two of you to help me."

The girls looked at each other smiling, and answered simultaneously, "We'll be here."

"Thanks girls. I'll see you then."

The last bell of the day rang and Mara and Val rushed to their lockers to put their books away. "What do you think we'll be doing?" Mara asked Val.

"I don't care. Do you know how envious everyone else in class will be because we were chosen to help her?"

"I guess. I'm just thinking it'll be fun."

They entered the room to find Ms. Karen opening boxes. She laid out some trays and scalpels.

"Girls, tomorrow we are dissecting frogs."

"Oh boy," Mara replied with her nose crinkled. She had already experienced dissecting and eating raw rabbit and that had grossed her out enough that she kept a good stash of beef sticks and snacks to keep the hunger and the wolf at bay. However, that was an experience she needed to keep to herself.

Ms. Karen laughed, "I think you'll find it interesting."

"I think it's gonna be cool," Val said as she reached over to pick up a bag of scalpels.

"You would," Mara laughed.

Ms. Karen handed Mara a tray lined with a paper towel, containing a small corkboard, straight pins and a scalpel, "I need both of you to prepare twenty-two more trays just like this one. When you're done place them around the lab tables for each student to have one tomorrow."

"Can do," Val said.

Ms. Karen sat down and graded papers as the girls completed their task. They boxed up the unused items. "Ms. Karen do you want us to put this away," Mara raised the box above the desk.

"No, I'll lock it in the closet in a minute." She wrote something before getting up and taking the box from Mara.

"Are you two in a hurry to get anywhere?"

"No Ma'am." Val answered.

"How would you feel about going and getting a sno-cone or something with me? I could really use some company for a while and you two can tell me about the town."

Val began to bounce giddily. She grabbed Mara's hand, "We'd love to."

As they left Sloopy's with their sno-cones, they saw Jenny leaving the courthouse. Mara hollered across the street to her, "Jenny," she waved for her to come over.

"I want you to meet our Biology teacher, Ms. Karen. She's new in town."

"It's so nice to meet you. You've certainly made a good impression with our girl," Jenny said as she hugged Mara to her side.

"Ms. Karen, this is my Aunt Jenny."

"It's nice to meet you too. I think I'm enjoying them just as much as they're enjoying my classes. I'm glad to meet you though. Being new in town, I don't really know too many people yet and if you don't mind it'd be nice to do something with you sometime."

"That'd be nice. I'm sure Mara gets tired of hanging out with me when I want to go shopping. We'll do lunch and the mall this weekend if you like?"

"Great, I look forward to it." Karen said as she handed Jenny a card from her handbag, "Here's my number. You just call me and we'll work it out."

"Sounds great to me, too." Jenny smiled and put the card in her purse, "It's been real nice meeting you."

Mara was happy to see Jenny and Ms. Karen making plans to get together because Mara knew that her time would be filled with Val and her new friends.

Chapter 21

Mara and Ray were on their way to the Norton's for their usual Wednesday night dinner date.

Ray had not seen any more signs of the creature responsible for Johnny's death. The time spent traveling to Jack's house always made him reflect on that night at the football field, the sight of Johnny's head and neck wounds. He had nothing else to report to Sheriff Norton that would help explain to Johnny's father what happened, and he refused to tell anyone what he had seen.

"Dad, are you okay?" Mara noticed the faraway look in his eyes.

"Yeah honey, I'll be fine."

"You just seem like you're somewhere else sometimes. I don't know, like you're worried or sad."

"I'm fine baby. Everything is just fine."

He didn't see any sense in telling her what was on his mind. It was good that the community and school seemed to be trying to move on and get things back to normal. He would be glad when he could also. If he ever could.

Once they arrived at Jack's, Ray noticed a strange car in the driveway. "Looks like they have company."

Mara grinned from ear to ear.

"What is it Mara?"

"Oh nothing. Just, you're about to meet Ms. Karen."

"The teacher you like so much?"

"Yep. Come on Dad!" She grabbed his hand and hurried him to the door.

"Okay, okay." He followed her to the door wondering what Ms. Karen would be like.

Jack answered the door with a proud smile on his face and led them into the kitchen. Standing at the bar with Jenny was a beautiful red head. Ray understood immediately why the kids liked her so much.

Jenny laid the pan from the oven on top of the stove and turned to face them, "Ray, meet Ms. Jayden, or Karen as she'd like us to call her. Karen this is Mara's father, Ray."

Karen Jayden held out her hand and Ray took it into his, "Nice to finally meet you. I have heard a lot about you."

"Likewise." Karen answered and smiled warmly.

Jenny didn't wait on an awkward silence, "Hope everyone likes lasagna."

"That's what smells so great." Ray remarked.

"She's been planning this night for a week, Ray." Jack grinned and gave Ray one of those looks that said it wasn't just the meal she's been planning.

"I'm pretty sure I'm gonna like it just fine." Ray replied with a smile on his face as he watched Karen and Mara in conversation.

"Good. Good." Jack said in approval. Jenny was nearly blushing at Ray's boyish smile.

She popped him on his backside with her dishtowel, "You stop it."

"What?" he asked innocently. "So far I like this plan. It's a beautiful distraction"

Jack sat the lasagna on the table as Jenny filled the tea glasses. They sat to eat but Ray could not take his eyes off Karen.

"I can understand why the kids like you so much," he told her as he reached for a piece of toast, "you are so youthful and beautiful."

Karen blushed, "You mean it's not because they enjoyed my classes so much."

"We do," Mara piped in.

"I try to teach them in a way that involves them and the more fun it is for them the more interesting and the better they learn. I just don't think there is enough student-involvement teaching anymore." She looked at Jenny for a nod of agreement.

"Well I sure could have used some teachers like you when I was in school." Ray stated, "I don't remember having any teacher as pretty as you."

Mara fidgeted in her seat, this was becoming a bit uncomfortable for her. She had never seen her dad flirt. Not ever. And she never thought she would, ever!

"Oh come on Ray," Jack said as he nearly choked on his tea," surely there was one teacher you had a crush on?"

"I can't think of one right now."

Jack noticed that Karen wasn't the only blushing face at the table. He had forgotten how shameless his old friend could be around a pretty woman. He cleared his throat, "Ray, ya care for a beer?"

"Sure."

Jack's chair scraped the floor as he pushed it back from the table, "Come on out to the patio and let's talk."

Ray followed Jack outside. Jack reached in the mini-fridge and pulled out two beers, handing one to Ray, he looked into his friend's eyes, "It's been a bit since Johnny's death. Have you learned anything else?" Ray raised one foot placing it against the brick wall behind him and leaned back into it.

"I have," he hesitated. He wondered how he should tell Jack about what he'd seen. He knew it would sound crazy, so he decided to keep it to himself.

"Well, ya gonna make me pry or are ya gonna spit it out?"

"I did manage to catch something in a trap. I don't know what because it carried the trap off."

"Carried the trap off?" Jack's voice pitched a little higher than usual. "Do you mean you didn't have it anchored well enough to contain whatever was caught in it?"

"No. It was anchored well enough," Ray walked away from the wall and sat in a chair across from Jack. "I'm gonna try again, but this time I'm gonna anchor the traps to trees."

"Mm, mm," Jack shook his head, "Must be some kind of beast."

Ray laughed nervously, "Yes, I think so."

"So long as you're still on it." Jack said in a way that let Ray know that people were still expecting some resolution.

"I am." Ray assured him, "I'll get it."

"Hey you think I got a shot with her," Ray said as he raised his beer toward the dining room.

"Fifty-fifty, far as I can tell. Ask her out." Jack stood and reached an arm across the back of Ray's shoulders in a buddy-hug.

Chapter 22

Skylar knew that if he and T.O. were going to get close
to Mara he would have to make the first move. He'd
always had a slight crush on Val but she'd been
Eddie's girl for the last three years.

He watched Val and Mara as they sat and ate their
lunch.

"T.O. let's go over there and say hi." He pointed
toward the girls' table and nudged his brother's tray.
"C'mon."

He stood with his tray and T.O. followed him across
the cafeteria.

Val was startled mid-sentence as a tray dropped on
their table. She looked up and saw the muscular,
blonde haired Skylar Owens smiling down on her with
his big brown eyes. She had noticed him at football
practices but she had been so wrapped up in Eddie
she never gave another guy a serious look.

"May we sit here?" he asked.

"Sure," Val said a little nervously, "if you want."

"We do," They sat and Skylar removed his utensils
from their plastic wrap, "I take it that things are over
between you and Eddie?"

"It would seem so," Val answered as she looked over at Julie and Eddie. She wished with everything in her that Eddie was paying attention to them right now. "Does that mean you might be open to a date with me?" he asked.

She looked back at him, "Mmm, let me think about it." He started to stand and she reached across the table and put a hand on his tray, "Don't go though."

He sat back down. "This is my friend, Mara." She looked at Mara, "and Mara this is Skylar Owens."

"I know your name," Skylar said to Mara, "but you probably didn't know me. It's nice to meet you."

"Nice to meet you too Skylar." Mara smiled and then she smiled bigger at Val.

"Mmhm." T.O. cleared his throat and Skylar laughed at his often-awkward brother. "Sorry bro. This is my brother T.O." T.O. raised his fork a few inches, "Hi." Skylar continued his quest with Val, "There's a hayride in a few nights and I really would like you to go with me Val."

Val blushed, "You know that would be nice. I was just going to skip it this year. I don't know though, I hate to leave Mara alone."

"No. You go." Mara's eyes widened at Val, "Don't sit around on my account when you could be on a date. Are you kidding me?"

"Well, it's just," Val looked down, "you've been so good to go through everything with me. I just don't want you to feel left behind or alone."

"Look girl, it's not a problem. It's a date right? It's not like you're just ditching me." Mara prodded, "I'm really happy Skylar here asked you out. You should go."

"There's no need for Mara to be excluded. T.O., ask the pretty girl to go with you."

T.O. looked at Mara with a slight blush in his cheeks and quietly said, "If she wouldn't mind?"

"No. I think I would like that very much." Mara replied happily, struck by T.O.'s shyness. It always concerned her that she would be too shy to get any guy interested in her and now it seemed she'd met someone shier than herself.

"Okay," Val smiled at Skylar, "It's a date then."

***

Mara and Val were at their lockers preparing to leave school for the day. Mara raised her books to put them in the locker when Val pushed her books to the floor. As Mara bent to pick them up, she saw another hand reaching for them. She turned her head and found herself looking into the emerald eyes of T.O., eyes so green, so wonderfully bright, she could hardly look away. She felt awkward that she had not given him a second look in the cafeteria.

Tyler noticed an innocence in her eyes and a poutiness to her mouth that made her look as if she were an angel. Something about her looked so soft and genuine, it stirred him even more than her hazel eyes surrounded by lashes as dark as her hair.

"Thank you." She whispered as she took the books from him.

Skylar held Val by her waist and turned her around. "So we were talking and we wondered why we should wait until the hayride to start having a good time. Do you think that you and Mara could meet us at the bike park in a little while?"

She shot Mara a sly grin, "We'd love to!"

Chapter 23

They arrived at the bike trails just in time to see someone come off the top of a hill and fly through the air for several feet.

"I hope they don't have any bright ideas about doing that with us." Mara said as she put the car in park.

"Where's your sense of adventure?" Val giggled.

As they got out of the car, T.O. rode up to the driver's side.

"Where is Skylar?" Val asked.

"Just came off that hill," T.O. pointed, "he'll be here in a minute."

They watched as Skylar brought the bike to a stop. He removed his helmet and placed it on his gas tank in front of him, "Hey, ladies."

"Hey, Skylar." They looked at each other and laughed. Their replies were often in unison and it only endeared and strengthened their friendship.

"Ya'll ready for some riding?" Skylar asked.

"Yeah but no jumping like you did," Mara replied.

The boys laughed. T.O. took her by a hand, assuring her, "No problem. You don't do jump that high with someone on the back of your bike."

"Just little hills," Skylar snickered.

"I don't mind any hills you want to take me over Skylar," Val purred as she climbed on the back of his bike and hugged up to him wrapping her arms around his chest.

Mara followed Val's lead, climbing on the back of T.O.'s bike. T.O. was careful with Mara but Mara was a bit envious of the laughter coming from Val and Skylar as they jumped some small hills and rode under some low branches. She wished she could be as carefree, but having a sudden brush with death shook that right out of her.

T.O. stopped the bike and turned his head toward her. "Wanna learn to drive this thing?"

"I don't know if I can."

"Sure you can. It's easier than learning to ride a bicycle."

"I guess I can try." Mara couldn't see how it could be easier than riding a bicycle but she was willing to try if that was what T.O. wanted.

T.O. shut down the bike and got off, he held it as Mara scooted to the front and he got on close behind her, keeping his hand on the left grip and grabbing the other as he got behind her. She could feel his breath on her ear and it caused a ripple of goose bumps to flow down her back, "Put your hands on the grips and pull the left handle in." Once she did it, he continued, "Good. Now put the toes of your left foot under the gear bar."

She looked down to see what he was talking about and she placed her foot as he'd instructed.

"Roll the bike slightly forward and pull up with your foot." She did. "Now, you are in neutral. You can release the clutch in your left hand and crank the bike by turning the key with your left hand and giving it just a bit of gas with your right hand by turning the grip in toward you."

She pulled the grip down and turned the key. The bike came to life, roaring beneath her. She shook a bit in excitement, and a little in fear, of this new experience. T.O. continued his instruction, "Now you know where the gears are, the clutch, the gas, your bar to the right that resembles the clutch is a brake for your front wheel. The gears are at your right foot and by your left foot is the brake for the rear tire. Do not brake your front tire without braking your rear tire some first. Got it all?"

"Yeah, I think so."

"Okay, pull in the clutch and bump the gears down as far as they'll go. Then release the brake and let off the clutch slowly."

She did as he said and a big smile spread across her face as the bike rolled forward. He talked to her as she drove, explaining as they went, when the gears needed to be shifted for each time.

"You are doing great. You're like a natural to this. Are you sure you haven't done this before?"

"No I never have." She laughed. She could get used to it though. It was a fun and free feeling and T.O.'s arms around her just added to her enjoyment.

They passed Skylar and Val on the way to the car and if a bug had wanted to, it could have had a sure chance at Val's tonsils as she gasped in shock at Mara driving the dirt bike.

Once they were all at the car and off the bikes, she hit Skylar on his arm. "Hey why didn't you teach me to drive?" Skylar laughed, "You scare me a little. You have no fear. But I guess if you want to learn I'll teach you next time."

"You be sure and do that."

"I will."

"We gotta head home for dinner." T.O. said as he took Mara's hand in his and they walked to her car.

"Yeah I guess we'd better head home, too." T.O. kissed Mara gently and opened her door. As she turned to get in, she saw Skylar holding Val's door. It was a wonderful afternoon and she hoped there would be more like it. This is how she wanted life to be, just normal.

Chapter 24

After homeroom Friday, T.O. met Mara at her locker,
"Walk with you to class this morning?"
"Okay."
He reached over and took her books, and placed them
on top of his books.
"How sweet and old fashioned. Thank you kindly sir."
"You are so welcome Madame." Then he smiled his
beautiful bright smile that made her want to pinch
herself in a reality check. She spent most of her time
that morning wondering where he had been all her
life. When class was over, he told her good-bye in the
hall and promised to see her at lunch.
They sat at the table discussing their plans for the
evening and Mara pushed her hair back from her face,
leaning into the table. She noticed T.O. looking at her
cheek and hated that she had not thought about it.
"Where'd you get that?" T.O. asked as he ran his
finger along the scar.
"Oh, it's silly really. Hardly worth talking about."
"Our girl here spent a week in the woods by herself."
Val spoke out with pride as if Mara had won some
kind of contest or something great.

"Really?" The boys asked simultaneously. They were very interested to hear about it and Val loved having their full attention, so she continued, "She went to the lake by her house in the middle of the night. It was dark and she got turned around and lost. But here she is. She found her way back!"

Mara was so embarrassed, "I hadn't been in those woods since I was a child. Of course I would forget my way and it was dark..." she barked defensively. How dare Val tell them that story. It made her look so stupid. It didn't matter it was a lie she had to tell but it was really nobody's business. She rose from the table throwing her chair back onto the floor and ran out the back door of the cafeteria. She could feel her eyes burning and hoped no one saw her. She ran for the woods with her head down and by the time she crossed the field and entered the trees, she had already shifted. She ran for a little longer and when she reached the creek, she quenched her thirst and tried to relax.

She knew she could not go back to school and she didn't know how she was going to explain this to her dad when he found out. After she calmed down, she walked slowly back toward school. She didn't know what condition her clothes would be in but she had to find them and she had to get home without anyone seeing her.

Her clothes were ripped so badly they were practically useless but she was able to cover enough of herself with the large parts of them so that she was not completely bare. She paused and looked up at the school from behind the trees. She didn't see anyone around outside of the building and she noticed where she parked her car behind the gymnasium was free from windows except for the locker rooms. She was almost certain there would be no one in there right now. She ran for her car, grateful that her dad made her keep a spare key in a magnetic box under the tire well.

When she got home, her dad's truck was there. She passed the driveway and rode around for a while trying to figure out how she was going to get into the house without him seeing her like this. She was already going to be in enough trouble for leaving school early. He didn't need to see her clothes all torn, how in the hell would she ever explain that to him.

She turned around and pulled into the yard trying to avoid the gravel. As soon as her car was off the road, she parked it. Her heart pounding as she sat there for a moment. Her muscles were beginning to contract but she focused on her breathing and envisioned her meadow. She couldn't afford to change right now. She looked around the outside of the house and saw no movement. Her dad would normally be in his study at this time of day and she hoped that was where he was now. She slowly got out of the car and quietly pushed the door closed. Then she bolted to the back porch. She pressed her body to the side of the house and listened through the screen door.

She could hear only her dad's voice and he sounded far enough away for her to surmise he was on the phone in his study. She quietly turned to the screen door and pulled it open. She stretched over to the counter with the top part of her body and reached to grab a rag to place in the doorway so that it wouldn't make a sound as it closed. She stood up straight and stayed still, listening. When she was sure he was still having a conversation in his study, she sneaked through the kitchen to the living room and scurried up the stairs to her room. She closed the door behind her and leaned against it.

Ray heard a sound as he hung up the phone. He walked to the living room and looked outside, not noticing anything at first, but then as he was about to close the curtain he noticed Mara's car at the end of the drive.

He looked up the stairs and saw that her door was closed, so he went up and knocked on it, "Mara, are you ok in there?"

"Yeah." Was all she replied.

"Why is your car at the end of the driveway in the grass?" He looked at his watch, "And why are you home an hour early?"

"Dad, I don't wanna talk about it right now." She answered.

"Well you need to get ready to talk about it. I want an answer young lady."

"I'll be down in a little while," she paused, "I'm just not ready to talk."

"Okay, I'll be waiting."

"Okay." She said softly, grateful he was willing to wait.

A few hours later she entered the kitchen, Ray stood at the stove cooking dinner. He turned off the stove and they sat at the table. Mara held her breath. She had decided to tell him the truth about what happened. Well, part of it anyway.

Ray looked at her and waited.

"Dad, there are these two guys at school and they really seem to like Val and me. Anyway at lunch today one of them noticed my scar and asked me about it." She took a deep breath and held strong to remain calm and not get angry with Val again. She had already practiced upstairs but wanted to proceed with caution.

"Well honey that's nothing to be ashamed of," Ray assured her.

"No dad. Val just had to go and tell them all about me getting lost in the woods. You know how stupid that makes me sound?"

Ray laughed, "Oh, baby. Look you made it okay, and after being out there for nearly a week. How many people do you think could survive that and find their way back?"

Mara shrugged her shoulders.

Her dad put a hand under her chin and lifted her face to his, "Not many. Listen I'm sure everything is going to be okay."

"But I was so embarrassed."

"Don't be. I understand you don't want to be embarrassed in front of your new friends but in the future, we'll have to find another way to deal with things like this. You can't just get up and walk out of school like that, okay?"

"Yes sir. Thanks Dad."

"You're welcome. Now go get your car and pull it up to the house, Karen is coming over to dinner tonight."

Chapter 25

Karen showed up at 6:00 and Ray yelled for Mara to come down. Then Mara panicked. She had forgotten that she and Val were supposed to go by Ms. Karen's classroom after school. She hoped she wouldn't have to tell Ms. Karen about her embarrassing day to answer for that. She put on a smile hoping it would seem like everything was fine and she'd done nothing wrong. She crossed her fingers that Ms. Karen wouldn't be upset as she opened the door and walked downstairs to the living room.
"Hey."
"Hey Mara. Is everything okay?"
"It is now," Mara smiled.
"Good. I was worried about you, but Val said she'd made you mad at lunch and that you'd left."
Ray stood in the kitchen door, "Dinner's done. Ya'll come on."
"Yeah, but I'm good now," Mara took Karen's jacket and hung it by the door before they walked into the kitchen.
"What are you two talkin' about?" Ray finished setting the table and sat down with them.

"I was just telling her I was glad she was doing okay now?"

Ray laughed, "Ya know, I can't remember ever leaving school because someone made me angry. Maybe I got into a fight a time or two and got sent home, but I just never ran out."

Karen put her hand on Mara's, "Girls are different, Ray. And besides, Mara was trying to control it. You know, not make it into a big fight or cause a scene." She looked at Mara, "Right?"

If she only knew, Mara shifted a little nervously in her seat, "Yes. I just needed to get away."

Karen smiled at Mara with a warmth and understanding in her eyes. Mara looked at her plate and shifted in her seat, somewhat uncomfortably. There was no way anyone could ever understand what she dealt with when her emotions got away from her.

"Well nevertheless, I've explained to her that she needs to find a different way to deal with these situations. After all, she cannot go through life running from every embarrassing or upsetting situation. She has to learn to talk and resolve her problems."

Karen patted Mara's hand, "Yeah, you're right about that." She continued to look at Mara, "She just needs someone whose, well a female, to help her learn to cope with those things the way she should. And I hope you know, Mara, that you can come to me if you need someone to help you."

"I will. Thank you." Mara said softly, still staring at her plate as Ray put a slice of meatloaf on it.

Just as they were beginning to eat, they heard the sound of motors out in the driveway. Mara rose from the table and stepped out onto the back porch. Two motorcycles and three people were approaching. She watched as they stopped and then she noticed Val's red sweater and on her shoulder was Mara's purse. Val got off the bike and removed her helmet. She walked up to Mara with her bottom lip poked out, "I'm sorry. I'm so sorry. Please don't stay mad at me."

"I'm not, it's just," Mara shrugged, "you really embarrassed me, Val."

"I know. You know me-foot in mouth syndrome. I just get excited and open my mouth without thinking things through or like, I don't know, letting you answer for yourself."

'Yes, I do know but to be honest it's your easy excitement that I love about you. It's just never been a problem for me before."

"I'll try to do better, okay?" Val looked up at her with a little pout, BFF's?"

"Yeah." They linked their pinkies and grinned at each other.

Val took the purse off her shoulder and held it out for Mara. "I tried to text you several times but then I realized I had put your purse in my locker, well you know, it was like, duh, Val."

Mara laughed at her and took her bag, "Thanks." She looked over at the guys, "T.O. and Skylar?"

"Duh, who elses?" Val smiled from ear to ear, "They think your survival story was awesome by the way."

Mara's dad stepped out from the screen door where he'd been listening. "Friends?" he asked.

T.O. and Skylar removed their helmets and got off their bikes.

Ray looked the boys up and down as Mara introduced them, "Dad these are the guys I was telling you about," she raised her hand toward T.O., "this is T.O."

Val stepped closer to Skylar, "And this is Skylar."
Mara wrapped an arm around her dad's, "This is my dad."
"It's nice to meet you. Just call me Ray. We were just about to have some supper, if you kids would like to join us?"
"Thanks," they replied.
Mara stopped at the back door once her dad had re-entered the kitchen. She turned and rolled her eyes at her friends, "Ms. Karen is here."
"You're kidding right?" Val tried to look over Mara's shoulder into the kitchen. She turned around, "Hey you guys, Ms. Karen's in there."
She turned back to Mara, "She was worried about you this afternoon, but I can't believe she drove out here to check on you."
"No she didn't." Mara's face flushed, "My Aunt Jenny introduced them to each other and well, they're kinda dating now."
"Whoa," Skylar grinned, "You're dad is dating the hot teacher?"
Mara shrugged, "Yeah, I guess he is."
"Well, I'm definitely in for some dinner." Skylar looked at T.O. as he reached around Mara and pulled the door open, "Come on bro."
Ray had already placed their plates and silverware on the table. "I was beginning to wonder if you guys were coming in."
Mara pulled three colas from the refrigerator and handed them each one, "We're here."
"I'm glad." Ray said as he began to pass the food

around the table. "Karen do you know everyone?"
"No, I haven't had the pleasure of these two young men in my class."

Ray held his fork and aimed it to his right, "This is Skylar," and flipping the fork to the opposite side, "this is T.O.." Then he chortled, "I'm sure I don't need to explain to them who you are."

"No sir." Skylar said just as he was about to insert creamed potatoes in his mouth. "Ow!" He yipped as T.O. kicked him under the table, "Have some manners man."

Everyone laughed then. "So, I guess everything is okay with you kids now?" Ray asked looking more to Mara for an answer than anyone else.

T.O. answered, "Yes sir. I'm not sure why Mara got so upset." He looked at her, "I think it's cool she did okay out there and managed to find her way back."

"Yep, she's pretty amazing." Ray glowed as he watched Mara take a drink of her cola.

They finished dinner and Ray began to clear the table. T.O. stood and picked up his plate, "Mr. Taylor?" Ray shot him a quick look, "It's just Ray, son."

"Yes sir, Ray why don't you and Ms. Karen go on in the living room and we'll clean the kitchen."

"Are you sure?" Karen asked.

"Yeah," he looked at Mara, "The four of us can have it done in no time."

Val agreed, hating that she wasn't the one to think of it first.

"Wonderful," Ray accepted as he took Karen's hand and led her from the kitchen.

"Way to score some brownie points you brown noser." Skylar teased once they were all alone.

"I just want to make sure he's gonna let me take Mara on the hayride tomorrow night, that's all."

Mara walked over to the sink behind T.O., "You want to take me on the hayride?"

"Yeah, I mean obviously your dad has to okay it first."

"I'm pretty sure you're right about that."

Val popped Skylar on the back of his head, "Aren't you gonna take me?"

"Of course." He said as he leaned over the table, took the last biscuit and devoured it.

Val picked the bowl up and handed it to Mara, "That's the last of them."

"Good, we can go watch T.V. with Dad and Ms. Karen after this." Everyone noticed the sarcasm in her statement.

"I don't know. I think it's kinda cool, hanging out with a teach away from school." Skylar noted.

"Who sounds like a brown-noser now?" T.O. smirked, "And bro, you don't even go to her class."

"No. But I wish I did." Val hip-bumped Skylar, then giggled. "Whoops, I didn't mean to do that. Should I be jealous?"

"No," Skylar turned her toward him and kissed her, "she'd never let me do this."

"Well, she don't know what she's missing." Val whispered.

They entered the living room to find Karen and Ray watching the Discovery channel. Mara sighed, "You guys couldn't find a movie or something."

"You know I love to watch the wild life programs." Ray reminded her. "Turns out Karen likes them, too. She was a Zoologist before she became a biology teacher."

"That's too cool," Skylar smiled at her.

"It was," Karen said, "but then I had to give it up."

"Why?" Val asked.

"Oh, personal reasons, if it's okay I really don't want to talk about it."

"Uhm, okay...." Val said accepting that she shouldn't push her curiosity.

"This is a pretty cool show though." T.O. said, "Check out those wolverines. They're so tough. They jumped right on that wolf. It's much larger than they are and they just tag teamed it."

"Educational and entertaining, right?" Ray pointed out in a question.

"Yes, it is." T.O. replied.

They finished watching in silence as the wolverine wrapped around the wolf's face tore into the throat of its victim and the wolverines took it down. Mara silently hoped there were none of those in their area, but she knew that was just as unlikely as the fact that she and her mother were wolves. But, oh yeah, they are...then she realized she'd probably be safe from that because she never intended to let the wolf in her take over again. There was no point. It wasn't going to bring her mother home and she had no intentions of living the life her mother lived.

The boys stood and Skylar helped Val up from the floor, "I guess we should be heading home now."

"It's been nice to meet you all," Ray shook their hands.

"Come on out with us Mara. "Skylar tilted his head towards the front door. Mara looked at T.O. who urged her on, "I'll be out in minute. You go ahead." Once Mara was out the door, T.O. sat on the edge of the couch next to Karen, and looked at Ray, "Do you mind if I take Mara on the hayride tomorrow night?"

"No, I don't mind. You just make sure you behave as nicely while you're out with my daughter as you did tonight?"

"Yes sir, I will." T.O. walked to the door and just before he turned the knob to open it, he turned back to Ray, "Thank you, Ray."

"No problem kid."

"I'm guessing from the grin on your face that tomorrow night's a go." Skylar watched his brother as he approached.

"Of course. Why would you ever doubt my abilities? You call it brown-nosing, I call it charm."

"Justify it however you want, man." Skylar laughed.

T.O. turned to Mara, "So, would you like to go on the hayride with me?"

"I would love to." She looked over at Val who was deep in a kiss with Skylar and when she turned back to T.O., she blushed in embarrassment. T.O. took her hand and kissed her on the cheek and sighed into her ear, "Awkward, huh?"

"Just a little." She whispered back but secretly she wished T.O. were kissing her. She wondered if anyone would find it unbelievable that she was truly sixteen and never-been-kissed.

She watched as they left and then ran into the house. Ray could see the excitement gleaming in her eyes as she thanked him before going up to bed.

Chapter 26

The Wilson farm was at the end of a long road, lined with cornfields on both sides. It was a beautiful night. The sky looked like a black wall with thousands of tiny holes which let light shine from somewhere behind it. Mara hadn't quit smiling since they'd left her house and her jaws ached, but she just couldn't quit smiling.

She couldn't remember the last time she was so happy. She ran through her mind trying to remember and then it happened. *Okay, it hadn't been that long ago.* It was when she learned her mother was alive, but that happiness had been short lived and replaced with another emotion. An overwhelming sense of guilt for what she had done the last time she even hoped for her happiness to last. The life she took trying to protect their secret and the sense of loss. Tears began to stream down her face and her smile faded. The sense of hope that anything in her life could ever be as normal as it seemed to everyone else was nonsense.

She let go of T.O., wiped the tears from her eyes and pasted a smile back on her face. She had to let go of that part of her past, forget and make the best of the rest of her life. Maybe tonight was a start. *Maybe,* a word so full of hope.

As they neared the barn she noticed several more cars there than just the ones that traveled the road with them. She leaned closer into T.O. and spoke loudly at the side of his helmet, "There's a lot of people here." He turned his head and hollered back towards her, "Yeah, it is."

They were able to park their motorcycles near the barn and as T.O. removed his helmet, he finished, "As you can see there is more than one wagon ready to haul everyone."

"I see," she said. She turned at the sound of Julie's voice. *But of course they'd be here,* she looked at Julie and Eddie hugged up to each other. She walked over to Val, "Are you okay?"

"Why shouldn't I be?"

"Have you not seen them?"

Val looked around and her head stopped when she spotted them. She hugged Mara, "You know what? I'm okay."

She stepped back and grabbed Skylar's hand. "Let's the fun begin!" She smiled at Mara, "We're gonna have a good time tonight."

Skylar was careful to choose a wagon separate from Eddie and Julie's choice. They settled in a far corner in the rear of the wagon and lay on the bed of hay with their heads resting on some partial bales.

Mara wondered how many stars there truly were in the sky and if there was even a numerical value in the human language to describe it. Infinity, no, that seemed more a measurement of length than of quantity. Soon her thoughts were interrupted as the wagon began to move. "Where were you just then?" T.O. asked her.

"In the stars."

He looked up at them, "I can see that. You are just as mysterious and beautiful as they are. Yep, I'd say you fit right in."

"Oh stop." She gently slapped his shoulder.

"What?" He laughed, "Am I embarrassing you again?"

"No, but don't lie to me. I know I'm not that beautiful. I'm pretty average, I know that."

"Just calling it like I see it."

Uneasy with his compliment she looked over at Val to draw someone else into the moment, but all she saw was the back of Skylar's head.

She sighed and looked back up to the stars. She could feel T.O.'s stare and she folded her hands on her lap.

"Do you think you might want to come back with me next weekend and go through the corn maze?"

"Sure. I mean, if you want to?"

"Why wouldn't I?" he asked.

"I don't know. I guess," she was stopped mid-sentence when T.O. tried to kissed her.

She turned her head away, surprised. "I'm sorry," he murmured.

"No." She looked at him, "You don't have to be. It's me. I just wasn't expecting you to do that."

"I guess I should have touched you first or something. I don't know it just seemed like the thing to do or something."

She looked down at her hands and unclenched them from each other. She placed one on his cheek, "Would you do it again?" she asked.

He leaned into her and softly placed his lips on hers and this time she kissed him back, falling into the niceness of it. Her first real kiss and it felt so sweet, she breathed in deeply and there was the scent of him, the hay and the night air. It was a more wonderful scenario than she had ever fantasized.

As T.O. held her tightly to him, she looked over his shoulder at Val and Skylar and understood. They were lost in time with each other, no pain, no worries, just pleasure.

She laid her back against T.O.'s chest and enjoyed the comfort and warmth of him as they returned to the barn.

Chapter 27

Ray watched as the kids took off on the dirt bikes.
Karen was out of town for the day and he decided now
was a good time to get his game cameras from the
shed and place them around the creek.
Jack watched Ray from his car as he exited the shed.
It had been several weeks since Johnny's death and
Ray still wasn't disclosing much information as to
what he intended to do to resolve the situation.
Jack wanted something more. The law side of him
needed more answers and the human side of him was
just curious as to all the secrecy.
He offered to help but Ray would not accept. He'd
replied only that he didn't want to interfere with
Jack's duties to law enforcement and since this wasn't
a murder, it shouldn't consume any of Jack's time.
But they both knew Jack wasn't that busy.
Basically, other than Johnny's death, there wasn't
anything on Jack's plate. The town was quiet, it had
been safe until this animal attack, and killing of a
citizen had occurred. He got out of his truck and
approached the house, waving to Ray, who was now
watching him. "What ya got there?"

Ray looked down at the game cams, "A couple of game cams."

"Ya got plans for 'em?" Jack stood with his hands on his waistline, a sign to Ray that he was there more on business than a casual call.

"I need to put them out there. You know. They'll give me eyes for what I'm trying to find. It's nocturnal."

"Oh yeah, what exactly is it?"

"Jack, I'm just not ready to tell you what I've seen. It's so unbelievable to me even. Short of sounding like a crazy man, the best thing to do, I decided is just to keep my mouth shut until I can prove it."

This did nothing but pique Jack's interest more.

"Let's go inside and I want you to tell me what's goin' on. I don't care how crazy you think it sounds, I need to know. I have to be able to tell Tom something before the town's men begin night hunting that thing. They get out there huntin' en masse in the dark, there's no telling what kind of accidents we'll have to deal with."

Ray continued to stand there, and again he looked at the cameras in his hands, "I'm on it Jack. I don't know what else to say." He pushed past Jack as he headed for the back door. Jack followed, "That's not good enough anymore. You are going to tell me something I can take back to Tom today. Now Ray, we've been pretty patient with you, but hunting season will be in full swing soon in a few days, and the whole town," his voice trailed off as he pulled a chair from the table. He sat and continued after drawing a quick breath, "they're talkin' Ray. They're saying that we're not doin' a thing to find that beast. Honestly, well, just tellin' 'em you're on it, that's just not any kind of answer for them. Not anymore."

Ray laid the cameras on the table and sat down. He looked at Jack and point-blank said, "It's a wolf." Jack laughed, "Oh come on now. There ain't no wolves round here. Whose leg you tryin' to pull?" "Seriously, it's a wolf. A Big One!" "And you're basing your belief of that on what?" "All the evidence at the scene of Johnny's death. I found the hairs on Johnny's body indicative of a wolf. But mostly the distance of length from paw print to paw print and the prints themselves." "You're kiddin' me right?" Jack said with a slight smile still on his face. Ray's face remained serious, which led Jack to believe he really wasn't kidding. "No. No, I'm not. And as if I didn't know it already, I saw it." "You saw it?" Jack said still disbelieving his friend. "I had a trap set up some yards off in the woods. I tracked it's travel trail from the school to an area back there," Ray lifted a finger and pointed out toward the woods along his property. "It was caught. I know it was because its howl woke me out of my sleep. But like I told you last week, by the time I got to the trap, it was gone and had dragged my trap off with it." "Ya planning to put any more traps out there?" "Not yet. If I could get a better view of what I'm dealing with..." his memory stopped him from continuing. He wasn't sure what else he could say. He couldn't tell anyone what he was dealing with. Not even his best friend. "Well, I'm just not sure a trap is the answer." "So, you don't think a tree will hold it? Must be some kind of outrageous idea you have for sure." Jack leaned all the way back in his chair and rubbed a hand across his face.

"No, not exactly. I mean I'm not saying that. I just need to know. Look I got this under control. I'll let ya know something as soon as I can get a shot of it."

"I certainly hope so. If I can't tell the town's men something soon, well, there's just no telling what kind of mess we're gonna have on our hands."

"Jack, look I promise you. I just need a little more time."

"I guess I'm gonna have to base my trust on our friendship because right now I'm not sure what's in that head of yours but I can see you're scared so I'll try to be patient a little longer. But I'm telling you Ray...."

"I know. I know." Ray stopped him. The two men moved back outside.

"I'm gonna let ya get back to it then. You call me later. Let's keep in touch better. I swear between this and that new woman I haven't seen or heard much of you at all."

"I know," Ray closed Jack's car door and tapped on the window a few times.

Chapter 28

Nora peered from the thicket at the wood's edge toward the lake, observing Mara and her friends. She had spent several times at this same spot over the years watching as Mara and her dad picnicked and fished.

Her daughter was becoming a woman, blossoming before her eyes in what appeared to be her first romance. She enjoyed watching the laughter in Mara's eyes and hearing it as T.O. held each other's hands and spun round and round.

She was relieved to see T.O. with Mara. She knew her child was safe with the Owens family involved.

She remembered the day she watched her little girl running and chasing butterflies. That day Mara got close enough to the bushes that their eyes had met and Nora had to bolt away.

She had no idea how she was going to re-open communication between them but she knew she had to do it somehow. She had to convince her to come into the pack. It filled her with sorrow to know what Ray would suffer and it broke her heart that she had to convince Mara to leave him. A whimper escaped out of her as she realized for the first time that she also robbed Mara of a life of normalcy. Ironically it was that very life she was trying to make sure Mara would have when she saved her.

It was too late now to regret any further. She had to turn it around, get Mara out of here or risk losing her for good. She had to clean up the mess she had made with her pack and protect her husband and her daughter from each other.

***

They decided to hang out at Mara's once they started losing daylight.

"Drinks?" Mara spoke over the boys chatter.

'Coke' was the unanimous reply. Mara went into the house and T.O. spun around to look at his brother, "Mara and I are going for a walk."

"Okay..." Skylar replied, wondering why T.O. was going to go off with Mara. Nevertheless, it meant he would have 'alone time' with Val.

Once Mara had passed every one's drinks around, T.O. grabbed her by her hand and tugged, "Come on, let's walk."

"Okay."

Once they were out of earshot of anyone else, T.O. dropped her hand and faced her. Mara I wanted to get you alone so I could tell you something, something only you can know."

Mara looked at him and saw the seriousness in his face, her smile faded. She couldn't believe he was going to share a secret with her this quickly. They barely knew each other. She worried he was getting serious too quickly. She wanted him to like her a lot. He was so beautiful and wondrous to her but she wanted things to develop in a gradual way. She had a secret too and she worried if things happened too quickly between them... well, like an argument of a serious nature or what would happen if things got too heated between them? She just didn't know and

it scared her, and now, already, he seemed confident
enough in their friendship to tell her a secret.
"Are you sure you want to tell me?" she asked
doubtfully.
"I don't just want to tell you, I need to."
"Okay then."
"I know your secret."
"What do you mean?" she asked defensively and in
disbelief.
"I know your mother, Nora."
Mara dropped to the ground and T.O. sat down in
front of her. Mara's eyes widened, "But how?"
"My family nursed her through a gunshot wound one
night after my brother and I found her in the woods.
We've been her friends ever since."
"But how do you know about me?"
"Your mother came to my parents weeks ago. She
was concerned for you because of the elders of the
pack. She refused to force you to come into their fold.
They think you are a risk for some reason.
She asked my mother if we could watch over you."
"How are *YOU* going to do that?" Mara couldn't
believe her ears. She had killed to keep their secret
and now her mother just goes and tells someone?
Incredible.
"My family, well, we're not exactly your average
family. We're all shifters."
"What?!"
"All of us. My mother, my father, Skylar and myself.
Generations before us even. We can shift into
any living creature we want to be."
"You're kidding me?" Mara's eyes widened with
shock.
"Would you like a demonstration?"

She looked up at toward the house and Val, "No, not right now."

"I understand." They stood up from the ground and T.O. reached for her hand, but she pulled it back.

"There's no need for you to act like you really like me. We can be friends and I don't want to pretend it's anything more."

T.O.'s feelings were hurt but he stayed silent, deciding that arguing with her would only aggravate the situation. He hadn't been pretending anything. He did like her a lot and he thought she liked him.

Mara was silent as they walked back to the house. Her hopes of a boyfriend dashed, all a ploy, a plot her mother put into action. She took a deep breath and held it for long moment, her mother didn't want to be here but it sure seemed like she was going to keep butting into Mara's life.

She let out her breath and looked at T.O. too upset to see the hurt in his eyes, "You know you really don't have to spend all your free time with me. My life has been just fine. My mother has just blown everything out of proportion."

They stopped just feet from Val and Skylar. T.O. looked up toward them and then at Mara, reminding her that the conversation needed to end. There were ears on the porch that didn't need to know about any of this.

When they got to the porch, Mara looked at Val, "Tell Skylar goodnight. They need to leave. I'll be in my room."

"Oh-kay." Val rose from the porch and gave T.O. a 'what's up' look. T.O. dropped his head and walked toward his motorcycle.

"What is wrong with you?" Val asked as she entered Mara's room and dropped back on her bed.

"T.O." was all Mara could say. She wanted to tell Val what was happening but she knew she couldn't. She had no idea how she was going to explain this to her. She had been so focused on not losing it that she hadn't considered Val's feelings.

"Is that it? That's all you're gonna tell me?"

"That's all I can tell you right now, Val. Just that, things aren't what they seemed to be."

"Well I don't know what happened with you but that was the nicest time I've had in months. Skylar is so funny and cute. He's a dream and I hope what you did tonight doesn't make him think less of me."

"That's right Val. Just turn into Julia on me. I just found out that the guy that I really like doesn't like me in the same way and you have to make it all about you." Mara's eyes filled with tears. Unsure if that was causing the burning sensation in her eyes, or if her emotions were bringing on the wolf, she quickly excused herself to go to the bathroom.

Once inside she looked in the mirror and saw the fierce orbs of blue in her eyes, she leaned against the wall and sank to the floor. This could not happen, not now. She ran to the meadow of her mind and swam in its waters until she was at peace.

Val sat in Mara's room and deliberated over Mara's words to her. It stung and she knew Mara was right and Mara helped her so much with her hurt over Eddie. She walked over to the T.V. and picked out a movie for them to watch on DVD. She realized how long Mara had been in the bathroom and became a little concerned. She knocked on the door, "Mara, you okay in there."

The knock brought Mara back to reality, "Uh, yeah. I'll be there in a minute."

"Okay. I picked out a movie, you wanna do that?"

"Sure."

When Mara entered the room Val apologized, "I'm so sorry and you are so right. No more about guys tonight. Just you, me and this funny movie."

She held up her pinky and Mara grabbed it in her own, "BFF's" they chimed. Then they made a promise to each other that no guy would ever come between them.

Mara spent most of the night trying to reconcile her new feelings toward T.O. and Skylar.

It would crush Val's happiness if Mara told her their relationships were just a ploy for her protection. Besides, how would she explain to Val why she needed their protection. What a mess life had become. She wished T.O. hadn't told her. She may have learned later that she had wasted her time on him but at least the time would have been fun and spent in blissful ignorance.

She didn't sense any danger and she hadn't been threatened by anyone. *Was her mother just concerned that she might kill someone else? Was the Owens family really there to police her?* She decided she didn't want to play the pretend game that T.O. started with her. She was done with him. It hurt but she had to take control of her own life now and allowing the situation her mother had put into place was not the way to do it. This seemed fair, the pain she felt. She had created so much misery in Val's life. She sighed, overwhelmed by her dilemmas.

She wondered if she would ever have a life of normalcy. After all her life had always contained mystery and now that she had the answer to the biggest question it was at the cost of her innocence. She realized now that no matter how

hard she tried, SHE was never going to be a normal
girl again. But she wanted it to be. She couldn't
believe her mother was continuing to interfere.
Her mother, ha, did she even deserve to hold that
title anymore. Mara was even angrier now with her
than she had ever been. She wasn't sure she even
wanted to see her again. She just wished the woman
would butt out of her life. Her father was lucky
enough to be done with her and he was happy now.
Mara wanted to be happy too and she was going to
find a way to do it.

****

T. Lee Moore is currently working on
"Consequences."
It is the next book in the
"Forever Changed" Series
Please visit her website to read excerpts from this
future story.

http://www.MooreGrimTales.com